# About the Author

He's a sixty-one-year-old machinist who has worked for the same company his whole life. He loves the outdoors, dogs, and skiing. He's a builder and a tinkerer. He never thought he'd be a writer. He didn't plan to write a book. The idea kind of found him! He had a very detailed dream. He woke up thinking, what a great scene that would be in a story. But, as dreams always work, he had no idea what events led up to this scene or how it ended. He was compelled to create the rest of the story! Enjoy!

# Bad Would Be Better

**Don Schrade**

# Bad Would Be Better

Olympia Publishers
*London*

**www.olympiapublishers.com**
OLYMPIA PAPERBACK EDITION



A CIP catalogue record for this title is
available from the British Library.

ISBN: 978-1-80439-229-4



First Published in 2024

Olympia Publishers
Tallis House
2 Tallis Street
London
EC4Y 0AB

Printed in Great Britain

# CHAPTER ONE

## MEET ANARCHY

No one would have, or could have ever imagined the perfect storm of events that led to the total collapse of society in our country. But so many things went so wrong, so quickly, that it resulted in the government, the economy, law enforcement, the military, and any sign of normal civilized life all falling into complete chaos, simultaneously.

There had long been a growing distrust for the government, especially among certain elements of society. But when the president, with only days left of his term in office, told a fanatical group of his supporters that the election had been stolen from him, their distrust went to a whole new level. Although the president had been repeatedly accused of telling endless lies to the people, spreading conspiracy theories, and fanning the flames of rebellion, his supporters continued to believe every word he uttered. When he told them to fight to get their country back, they felt emboldened and encouraged to take their president's words literally as marching orders to mount a direct attack on their nation's Capital. Shocked that this could happen even once, the American people thought that this was a one-off sort of event. They hoped that cooler heads would prevail once the newly elected president was in office. However, the damage had already been done. Once likeminded groups across the country saw what had unfolded in the nation's Capital, they decided to engage in similar attacks on not only the federal government, but on state and city governments, as well.

Ultimately, it turned out that there were many more radical groups, with larger memberships than previously thought, and they did indeed engage in more violent attacks on city, state and federal governments. It was thought that these groups may have had help from the inside. How else could they have so easily gained access to government buildings? Security? Military? Police? Government employees? Someone must have been helping them, but who? After all, these extremists had come from all walks of life, including former military and law enforcement. Did they have friends on the inside who were sympathetic to their cause? Eventually, after countless, increasingly more violent attacks, the government had suffered damage that could not be undone and eventually crumbled.

The pandemic had started about a year earlier and although quick progress was made in developing vaccines, getting them to the people had proven to be a more difficult process than expected and took much longer than expected. Many people refused to get vaccinated even once vaccines were available to them, either because they didn't trust the vaccines themselves, or because they thought it was some sort of conspiracy orchestrated by the government. Before the vaccines could be widely distributed, new strains of the virus were already coming along and the vaccines hadn't even been completely proven effective against the original strain. Eventually, the pandemic brought the whole world to the brink of economic collapse. The economy was severely weakened in much less time than it would take to recover. The stock market rallied, not due to real economic rebound, but because the wealthy and ultra-wealthy continued to throw money into it, which gave the appearance that things were much better than they actually were. This was not sustainable, and eventually, the reality of people losing jobs, businesses closing, and so many industries facing long term slowdowns and shutdowns caused the economy to crash, and the stock market with it.

The military, now without any official leadership, since the government was practically non-existent, fell into disarray. Some continued to fight for what the constitution stands for, while others broke away to fight for their own agendas. Law enforcement agencies went much the same way. A certain percentage of law enforcement were never on the right side of the law to begin with. They went off and looked out only for their own interests. The good that were left continued to defend what is right. They did their best to protect those who needed to be protected. But they faced an increasingly difficult challenge. They were soon to be grossly outnumbered and outgunned by the gangs and wannabe gang bangers, the radical groups and extremists hell bent on dismantling the government, and seemingly regular people who went beyond trying to survive and instead, let greed and opportunism turn them into ruthless animals who wanted to take much more than they needed no matter what it took or who it hurt.

The gangs in our major cities have long awaited such an opportunity. They have always believed that they should control the entire city in which they live. But they had previously been mostly contained in their neighborhoods by law enforcement. But now there was not much holding them back. They grew their numbers with anyone who would join them and eliminated anyone who wouldn't. Some gangs went to war against one another in an attempt to gain sole control.

Others formed alliances and joined forces to try to take over their cities. Eventually, the warring between gangs mostly ceased. The leaders of some of these gangs set up meetings where they agreed to work together and form "super gangs". It was unheard of for them to cooperate, but they knew they could be more powerful if united as one. They acquired the weapons, equipment, and manpower to overwhelm prisons to break out their allies from within those facilities.

They had managed to recruit skilled snipers who had previously been members of the military or law enforcement, but who had now changed sides due to extremist ideals they had been harboring within themselves up until now, or due to the fact that they had simply given up on the government already, long before all of this began. Still don't think this is possible? Maybe a couple of examples will help. Take Carl Jones. He was top of his class in sniper school during his time in the military. He did two tours in Afghanistan. It's not easy to end a life, even if it is someone who will certainly kill you or your friends if you don't take them down. It's bad when it's an obvious enemy soldier. It's much worse if it's a woman or even a child with a bomb strapped to their chest. He was forced, more than once, to make the decision to pull the trigger with a woman or child in his scope. He came home with a lot of guilt and the demons within him were tearing him apart. But getting the help he needed would cost more than he had and getting the government to assist proved to be next to impossible. In his view, the very government he fought so hard to protect was now leaving him high and dry. Eventually, he basically threw his hands in the air and said, "What the hell! The side I was on doesn't give a shit about me. Fuck 'em!" Then there's Emanuel Sanchez. He's one of the best snipers the SWAT team has ever had. For years, he's turned a blind eye to the fact that his brother-in-law is in a gang. He's a really bad guy. He's hurt a lot of good people. But if Emanuel tries to bring his brother-in-law to justice, he may lose his wife. The gang might take revenge by hurting his kids. As the gangs grow in power - and it's basically open season on anyone in law enforcement - he fears that if he stays in law enforcement, the gangs may come after him or his family, anyway. So, as a way to preserve the safety of those he loves, he reluctantly switches sides. These are only two examples. There are so many more highly trained, highly skilled individuals, formerly from a background of military or law enforcement, who made similar choices. So, yes, the gangs have plenty of snipers entering their ranks.

Once these sharpshooters had taken out the guards in the towers and at the gates, they would use heavy equipment which they had commandeered to break down the fences and walls. Then, through the sheer power of their numbers, they would overwhelm the remaining staff trying to contain the prisoners. Any of their allies doing time in the prisons were now back on the streets, as well as plenty more bad guys willing to join their cause. They are an ever-growing threat as they increase their numbers.

What's left of good, decent law enforcement and military personnel, along with ordinary people who possess the ability and will to do so, do their best to keep them contained, but they are losing ground. The gangs and the turf they control are growing like a cancer.

The rules have changed. No. There are no rules. It's every man for himself. Kill or be killed. The unarmed are quickly eliminated for whatever they have that is deemed to be useful to the thugs who kill them. Hospitals, clinics, and pharmacies are raided, killing healthcare workers and patients alike to get the drugs and medical supplies. Breweries and distilleries are seized by the gangs and kept running under their control. The warehouses full of alcohol are fiercely guarded by them as well. They want it for their own consumption as well as for a form of currency to get other things they need. Marijuana growing facilities and dispensaries are also taken over by the gangs, and controlled by them in much the same way. Factories producing everything from food, to weapons and ammunition, to drugs and medical supplies are seized by, and kept in operation, under the control of the gangs.

Even otherwise decent, law-abiding citizens eventually have to resort to whatever is necessary to survive. You can no longer go to a store and buy what you need. If you're able to find anything you need left there, you must just take it. But there isn't likely to be anything useful left. These places have mostly been looted for anything of value. So, the only remaining thing to do is find someone who has what you need. If you're lucky, and you have something they can use, you may be able to trade for what you need. But this can be dangerous because once they know you have something they want or need, they may just kill you and take it. Likewise, you may have to kill them to defend what you have and to get what you need. There aren't many friends in this new "society".

With the collapse of the economy and stock markets crashing, money has little value. If your only weapon happens to be a slingshot, coins make great ammunition! Paper money makes great kindling if you need a fire to keep warm. Guns, ammunition, medical supplies and drugs, alcohol, and food are the new currency. People without weapons don't stand a chance. And thanks to the anti-gun politicians, who have relentlessly tried to take guns out of the hands of law-abiding citizens for years, many decent citizens are without any way to defend themselves.

Remember the old saying, "If you outlaw guns, then only outlaws will have guns"? Only now are people realizing the true meaning of that old saying! So, they offer assistance to, or barter with, those who have them in exchange for weapons that can be used for defending themselves.

Everything is valued in relation to its usefulness, not what the dollar value once was. For example, even food is valued by how portable it is and how long it will last. Portability is important because you have to keep moving. And everything you need must be carried with you at all times. You will quickly be killed for whatever you have so you must be able and willing to kill quickly to defend it.

People do band together into small groups to help one another, but it is not easy to gain the trust required for this to work. You never know if someone is going to act like your friend and later turn on you to take your life and all that you have. You must be extremely careful and vigilant. Keep one eye on your enemy and the other eye squarely on your friend!

People become desperate. In order to survive, they find themselves killing someone while simultaneously apologizing for doing it. But oddly, everyone understands the situation so well that the apologies are often accepted. In many cases, it is almost looked upon as a form of mercy killing. Some people are almost glad it is ending for them because the world has become such a miserable place to be. They just couldn't bring themselves to end it themselves but the end is almost welcomed.

This is the new reality. No one is there to protect you. If you don't have the ability and strength to protect yourself, you're screwed. If you have what you need to survive, you must guard it with your life. If the ever-growing evil comes your way, you must either run or hide or be prepared to fight. To say things were bad would be a huge understatement. Things would need to improve, vastly, to be just "bad"!

# CHAPTER TWO

## MEET THE ENEMY

Some would say that the "bad" people would be so outnumbered by the "good" people that they couldn't possibly take control of our cities or our country, for that matter. But they don't see the whole picture. Let's break it down to make it understandable how the numbers of "bad" people can be so much larger than anyone would have dreamed.

The attack on our nation's Capital brought the radicals and extremists to our attention in a way they had never been before. Sure, we knew they existed, but they were never taken quite as seriously as they were being taken now. Suddenly, they were seen as a very real threat to our nation's security. If they could forcefully make it inside the Capitol and the Senate chambers and offices of government officials, where else might they be able to force their way into? Quite a few other places, it turns out! The state governments, as well as the governments of our major cities, were also attacked by these groups. This created chaos. People became afraid to even go to work in these places where they had previously felt safer than anywhere else. So, eventually, all forms of government were weakened to the point of not being able to function.

The effects were magnified by the fact that there have always been individuals who weren't part of any group or organization, but who had radical ideas, nonetheless. These people had anti-government and anti-society tendencies, but rarely acted on them. They always believed that “Big Brother was watching”, or that their government was “out to get them”. Some had engaged in mass shootings and bombings in the past, but most only thought about doing such things. Now, however, with security being almost non-existent, many of them engaged in lone wolf attacks on government buildings and law enforcement facilities, from shootings to bombings to just joining in with whatever the other extremists were doing.

With all of this keeping what was left of law enforcement and the military occupied, the gangs had very little resistance to run amok in their neighborhoods. They killed anyone who tried to get in their way. They destroyed and looted their own neighborhoods and when they had finished their devastation there, they began to expand their “turf” in all directions. They began to take over areas closer to the hearts of the cities. They also began to work their way out into the suburbs. As this expansion progressed, they soon realized that it would take more manpower to control the additional area. This is when the individual gangs started to do something completely unheard of. They began to join forces.

The wannabe gang bangers, who although they have no actual gang affiliations, from the nickel and dime drug dealer on the corner, to the neighborhood thugs who drive around shooting up neighborhoods just to be “hard” and “tough”, are all just a step away from becoming true gang members. They’ll kill you just for looking at them the wrong way. They’ll have no remorse for taking a life over a gold chain around someone’s neck that they want for their own. They might just “bust a cap” on you for being in “their territory”. The real “gangstas” are their heroes. How hard do you think it would be for an actual gang to recruit them into the ranks of their "soldiers"?

Not hard at all, really. Some would consider it the highest honor! So, it's no surprise that they, eventually, were recruited by the new "super gangs".

The police have some very good people in their ranks who truly are there to protect and to serve. Unfortunately, there are some that are not so good. Some work right alongside the criminals in exchange for a cut of the action. Greed gets hold of people in all walks of life and there are police officers who just can't resist using their position to line their pockets. They form alliances with everyone from drug dealers to organized crime. Whose side would they take when things fell apart? As if that's not bad enough, you then have the cops who only became cops to put on a uniform and carry a gun to be real "tough guys". They are even lower than the ones who let greed dictate their actions. The greedy ones are bad for sure, but one can understand their motives. It's much harder to understand why someone wants to "look" the part of what is supposed to be the good guy for such a stupid reason as to be able to manhandle and even hurt or kill the very people you swore to protect. The image won't go away. A cop, kneeling on the neck of an unarmed man, with his hands in his pockets, and his "joe cool" shades up on his head, and a half-assed smirk on his face like he was posing for a picture, as the man under his knee was dying. It was like a big game hunter posing for a photo with the trophy of a lifetime! It was enough to make you see your lunch for a second time. How many more unarmed people have been killed by trigger happy cops who just couldn't wait for the chance to fire their weapon at a real live target? Too many! They often say that they thought they saw a weapon so they were simply defending themselves. But, all too often, there is no weapon and they just let the adrenaline overwhelm their judgment. And is it really necessary for a cop, or several cops, to unload their weapons into a human being with kill shots instead of just enough wounding hits to disable the perceived threat? Part of being a good cop is accepting the possibility that you could get injured or even killed in the line of duty. No one would expect a cop to not defend himself appropriately, but that doesn't mean multiple kill shots before a threat has even presented itself. Anyone who can't accept that should look at another line of work. So, is it any wonder that some of these cowards ended up on the wrong side of the law when the "good" side wasn't winning?

The military isn't immune to these issues, either. There are many good, brave, and selfless people in all branches of our armed forces. And they make a lot of sacrifices for their country.

Some make the ultimate sacrifice. They deserve our gratitude and respect. But, unfortunately, this group of people, like any other group, has a certain percentage of its members there for the wrong reasons. Some sign up because they feel they will end up in prison if they don't. Some just see it as a way to get an education on Uncle Sam's dime. Most are willing to fight for what's right at any cost, while others may not hold up so well when the stuff hits the fan. They may either just leave and look out for themselves, or end up changing sides entirely. So, with little to no leadership to guide them, unfortunately, many do become part of the disease rather than part of the cure.

There are some of our own citizens who have been

"radicalized" by terrorist organizations from around the world. Some have actually left our country to train with them and fight alongside them. Scarier still, some are still here. Since 9-11, government agencies have closely monitored for "chatter" on all forms of communication to watch for possible threats from within as well as from outside our borders. But with very little government left, there are not so many watchful eyes upon them, nor ears listening for them. Some of these terrorist organizations have always hated the US and have been biding their time for another opportunity to attack us on our own soil. They are watching for that chance and some of their radicalized friends in the US will be all too happy to aid them in getting more of their people over here. Eventually, some of them do make their way onto US soil and add further to the attacks on our country and on those who are still trying to protect it. They bomb government facilities, financial institutions, and anything else that stands as a symbol of our country's wealth or strength. The US is less popular than ever with the rest of the world so there are even more threats out there. And our allies are less likely now than ever before to lend a hand when we are in turmoil.

We always knew that there could possibly be operatives of ISIS, the Taliban, Al Qaeda, or other similar terrorist organizations embedded within our own borders, just waiting for the opportunity to attack us on our own soil, again. They had managed to do it before, after all. Individuals from all over the globe had taken up the cause for these groups and been trained by them. They walked among us, working ordinary jobs, living in ordinary homes, and blended in perfectly. They had been trained to do or say nothing which might flag them as terrorists. And they did so, flawlessly. What no one knew was just how many of these people there were, hiding in plain sight. When things started to fall apart, that was their cue to come out of the woodwork and inflict as much damage as possible. And come out of the woodwork they did, in numbers that were unimaginable.

So many regular, civilian citizens have become desperate to survive. Some are driven to take what they need from others by force if they have to. They are forced to defend themselves, their families, and their property by any means necessary. This has otherwise ordinary people killing one another at an alarming rate. These people, under normal circumstances, would have never inflicted harm on anyone.

But the circumstances are anything but normal. When it becomes a matter of survival, people will do things they would have never dreamt of doing before. They suddenly find that they become willing to kill to get what they need or to protect what they have or those they love.

So, the attacks on our very society are coming from all sides. The major cities have become war zones. The suburbs beyond are little better, but the situation there is deteriorating rapidly. As people flee these areas, trouble follows them. The rural areas are relatively safe for the time being. But, in time, that may not always be the case. Some people in these areas have built well protected bunkers, stocked with emergency supplies such as food, water, medicine, weapons and ammunition, and anything else that would be needed to sustain themselves for a long period of time, in the event of some sort of emergency or disaster. They will thank themselves for being so prepared, soon enough.

It was like watching atomic bombs going off in every

major city, at once, in slow motion, and then watching the fallout spread slowly but steadily across the rest of the country. It was hell!

So, taking all of these factors into consideration, it turns out that there are a huge number of people and groups of people who are either directly or indirectly contributing to the destruction of our country. It's almost inconceivable, just how many people the "super gangs" are able to recruit. Some join them out of fear, feeling that they must either join them or be killed. Some have always wanted to rebel against authority, but, until now, would have had to do so on their own. Some have been desperate, all of their lives, to be part of something, and see this as their opportunity. Herd mentality takes over, just as it does when a few people engage in destructive activity, and before you know it, you have a full-blown riot on your hands. The extremists, radicalists, and terrorists think they are acting on their own, and would never consider themselves to be part of the "super gangs", but whether they realize it or not, they are part of the same movement. Every good person they kill and every government building they destroy only serves to clear the way for the gangs to expand and grow. It starts out slowly at first, but as the good citizens are either killed or forced to flee, and the evil of the gangs, radicals, extremists, terrorists, and others who have simply changed sides continues to expand, it snowballs into absolute mayhem and anarchy.

# CHAPTER THREE

## MEET SONYA

Rewind to nearly two decades earlier. A young sailor spending time in Puerto Rico meets a beautiful young woman there and they fall in love and eventually marry. They make a home in the US and soon welcome their first child, a girl, and name her Sonya. When her father is able to be home, he is an excellent husband and father. But the Navy keeps him busy so several years pass before they eventually have two more children, another girl and a boy. Sonya helps her mother take care of her little brother and sister while her father spends more and more time away. He enters Seal training and completes it at the top of his class. After becoming a Navy Seal, he goes away on many deployments all over the globe. He is one of the best of the best.

He loves all three of his kids but Sonya is always his favorite. In Sonya's eyes, Daddy is her hero. She inherited her mom's good looks and he knew the boys would someday take an interest in her. So, he taught her at an extremely young age how to take care of herself. By the time she was nine years old, she knew plenty of moves that would leave any unruly boy lying on the ground moaning in pain.

As she got a little older, she had plenty of chances to put what her dad had taught her into practice. And she was good at it. She had quick hands and feet, and she even took some

Martial Arts classes which made her an even more formidable foe for anyone who was foolish enough to mess with her.

By the time she was seventeen, her dad had left the Seals. He had done and seen so many horrible things that it totally changed him. He suffered from PTSD and depression and had awful nightmares almost every time he went to sleep. He became a withdrawn man with a severe drinking problem. When he was sober, he was still a good husband and father and continued to provide for the family. Unfortunately, he wasn't sober often. Alcohol, to him, was like Dr. Jekyll's potion. He became a real Mr. Hyde. He began beating Sonya's mom for seemingly no reason at all. It was like he was taking all the pain from his past out on her. Sonya and her mother convinced him to go get help. He saw a therapist a few times but he said it was a waste of time and stopped going. So, the drinking and the abuse continued.

Sonya couldn't bear to see this go on any more. So, one time when he began being violent towards her mom, she told him to stop and just leave. He didn't.

She said, "Okay, I warned you."

He said, "Oh yeah? What are you gonna do about it?"

There were no more words. Here was a man who had killed men with his bare hands. He was about to have his ass handed to him by an eighteen-year-old girl. She didn't want to do it. This man was once her hero. But she would not let her mom be hurt anymore. She beat him to within an inch of his life. He stumbled away with his tail between his legs and never came back. Her mom told her she shouldn't have done that because now there was barely enough money to feed her and her little brother and sister. Sonya told her, "We will make it work. No money is worth getting beat up like that. I will find a way to help."

Sonya's mom would have gladly taken the daily beatings if she would have known what her daughter was about to do in order to help feed the family. But Sonya kept the truth from her mom and simply told her she found somewhere to work part time. In reality, she began running drugs for a local gang. She wasn't really a "member" of the gang, in her mind. She was just working for them. The gang didn't quite see it that way. They placed more and more demands on her and told her what she would and would not do. Many of them tried to make her do things she simply would not do. And she put a few of them in their place. She could hold her own against one of them at a time, but eventually she was repeatedly and brutally abused by several of them at a time, both physically and emotionally. She was the gang's property. She was battered and bruised, but she would not be broken.

This was about the time that the country was falling apart and the gang had set its sights on taking over the city. This took some of the attention off of her and she wanted out. If there was ever a time to make a run for it, this was it. So, she disappeared into the night and made a break for it. She had to get far away as quickly as possible, but not before seeing her mom. She began explaining to her mom what she had really been doing, but her mom already had a pretty good idea since she had barely ever been home any more. She apologized to her mom for getting involved in such a bad thing. Her mom begged her just to come back home. Sonya explained that she couldn't do that. The gang would come looking for her and it would put her in danger as well as her little brother and sister. She said she had to go. She promised that someday, she would return for them. She had no idea if that would ever really happen. So, with a heavy heart, she left, hoping that they would be alright.

Fortunately, for Sonya's family, there were small groups made up of former military and law enforcement who had taken it upon themselves to go in and save people like them who had no way out and would otherwise be doomed. These people had the skills to do it and, somehow, needed a mission - something good to fight for. It gave them a purpose. It gave them hope. They couldn't save everyone but they could save some. One such group, within just a few weeks of Sonya's departure, got her mom and two siblings out of there and delivered them somewhere safe, or at least safer than where they were.

Sonya thought about her family all the time and worried about them. She knew in her heart that it was highly unlikely that she would ever be able to return as she had promised and she felt a lot of guilt for leaving them behind. She had no way of knowing that they had been rescued and did not know if she would ever see them again. It left a really empty place inside her.

She travels alone. She will need help, along the way, to make it to safety, even though she won't admit it. But she has no way of knowing who she can or can't trust. There are many obstacles for her to overcome. Her own gang wants to stop her. Rival gangs want to take her.

Seemingly normal people might try to take advantage of her situation to act like friends only to later turn on her. She sees that her good looks are a liability rather than an asset, so she does her best to not be noticed. She has learned to trust no one.

Sonya heads out on her own with nothing more than the

clothes on her back. Ever since she drove her father away, every penny she had went to feeding her mom and her little brother and sister. She didn't have enough left to be able to afford a phone. The gang had always supplied her with one, but only for doing their work. Once she escaped, that phone was cut off. It wasn't like a phone would have been much help, anyway. The people you would normally call for help weren't answering calls, any more. She was scared, hungry, and totally on her own.

Getting away from the danger surrounding her was a daunting task. She would sometimes only cover a few blocks per day. Patience was not easy but it was absolutely necessary. She had to move stealthily. Before making even the smallest move, she had to thoroughly scan the area to be sure no one wanting to hurt her would be alerted to her presence.

# CHAPTER FOUR

## RAPHAEL, MEET SONYA

Sonya uses the cover of darkness to travel at night and must find places to safely hide during the day. Progress is painfully slow, but she must be careful not to be noticed. She has no weapon. She has witnessed so much death from guns that she can't bring herself to carry one. She does know how to fight, but fists and feet are no match for thugs with guns. So, confrontation is avoided at all times.

One night, as daylight is rapidly approaching, Sonya must find her hiding place for the upcoming day. She finds a dark corner in an abandoned factory which has been thoroughly looted for anything of value. This is exactly what you want. If there is nothing of value, you are much less likely to have any unwanted company show up. She quietly, and very carefully, rearranges a few things to make her little hiding spot more secure and less likely to be noticed. She lies there for a bit and just listens. Total silence. Perfect! After a fair amount of time has passed with no sound whatsoever, she settles in to try and get some sleep. She needs the rest in preparation for the night ahead when she will repeat the same process she has been doing night after night for a couple weeks, now. That is, quietly and stealthily sneaking through the darkness to gain whatever distance she can away from the center of the city. She figures that in a few more nights, she could actually make it to the suburbs. This will be a huge improvement, as the farther she gets from the inner city, the less trouble she should have. The situation behind her has deteriorated quickly. Ahead of her is only slightly better, but better, nonetheless. As she lies there, planning her next night's movement, she begins to drift off to sleep.

Suddenly, she is startled back awake by the sound of a muffled sneeze from somewhere in the very room she is in! "Oh, shit!", she thinks to herself. She has become an expert in stealth, and decides it is better to find this other person before they find her. She makes careful note of the direction the sound came from, and silently waits for several minutes before moving to investigate. Upon hearing nothing more for several minutes, she is satisfied that this unwanted company has not moved. She very slowly, quietly, and methodically sneaks in the direction she had heard the sound come from. Since she had intentionally picked a room with no windows or skylights, it is unbelievably dark, which is good if you are hiding. But it's also bad for moving around quietly while trying to find something, or someone! She thinks to herself, "I'm sure glad Mom always made me eat my carrots! I need all the night vision I can get!" Sonya makes it to a position where she can just make out someone lying there behind an overturned workbench. Keeping the element of surprise on her side, she spots an extension cord and picks it up. In one smooth and lightning-fast move, she manages to loop the cord around the neck of this unknown man before he has any clue what is happening.

"Who the fuck are you?" Sonya snarled.

In an understandably raspy voice came the half-choking reply. "I'm Raphael. Who the fuck are you?"

Sonya said, “Never mind who I am. What are you doing here?”

“I was here first, remember? I could ask you the same. And if you could ease up a bit, I could talk a lot easier”, Raphael said.

She let up on the pressure, but just barely.

Raphael, sarcastically, said, “Gee thanks, that’s much better. Looks to me like we are both hiding from someone. Who are you hiding from?”

Sonya said, “None of your business. Who are you hiding from?”

He said, “I’ve been living the gang life since I was a kid. I’ve had enough. I’m getting out.” The cord loosened slightly since what he said really hit home with her. Then he said, “You sure aren’t sharing much about yourself.”

To which she replied, “Yeah, trust issues. All you need to know about me is that I am trying to get out of this hell hole.”

He said, “You gotta trust someone, sooner or later. You’ll never get through this alone.”

She said, “Well I got this far, didn’t I?”

What he said next made her realize that she had much farther to go than she thought. He said, “The gangs have expanded all the way out to many of the suburbs, looting homes and businesses all along the way. And they are killing anyone that gets in their way. The last of the police and military who have been trying to hold them back have been pushed all the way to the outer edges of the suburbs. And they are having a hard time holding on. Some citizens are joining forces with them and helping however they can, but it isn’t enough.”

Sonya asked, “How do you know all of this?”

He said, "Because I've been out there."

She asked, "If you've been out there, why in the hell are you back here?"

He replied, "I came back to save a friend."

"So, where is this friend?" she asked.

He hung his head and said, "They killed her three days ago. I couldn't get to her in time. So, there's nothing left for me to do here. I'm heading back out, this time for good."

The cord around Raphael's neck loosened completely once Sonya had heard his story and could tell it was completely true. She said, "So, you know your way back out, then?"

He nodded yes and said, "You are very pretty, by the way." SNAP! The cord was now tighter than it had been before! "Whoa, easy", he gasped.

"Don't get any ideas, got it?" she said.

"Okay, okay", he said.

Sonya had released Raphael and moved off a short distance to calm down and try to stop shaking. But she kept a very close eye on him. Eventually, he worked up the courage to approach her to talk some more.

He asked, "You got a name?"

She replied, "'Hey You' will work just fine for now." Then she asked, "So, what's in that backpack that you seem so attached to?"

He said, "You learn real fast what you need and what you don't. And you learn to never let it out of your hands. It's just the essentials. Enough food to get by until you find more, some basic first aid stuff. Some medicine if you're lucky enough to have any. Anything that could be of value to trade with someone for something you may need. Whatever you can carry that won't slow you down or make noise. You always keep your eyes open for supplies. Pick up what you can and keep it in your pack, which, by the way, you should get for yourself ASAP. Sometimes it's a long time between finding useful items, so you need to have some with you at all times. We'll find you a pack."

"We?" she asked.

"Yeah, I will help if you let me," he said.

Sonya had not trusted anyone for a long time, especially any man. But she somehow knew Raphael was different. She could hear the sincerity in his voice as he shared his story. However, old habits die hard and she still didn't trust him. But he knew how to get out of the danger zone, or at least most of the way, which was more than she knew. And he seemed willing to let her tag along. Maybe he even actually wanted to help her. She knew any help was better than trying to find her way on her own.

Sonya asked, "How do I know I can trust you?"

Raphael said, "Look, you might not want to tell me what your story is, but I know that we are both trying to do the same thing. That is to get out of here, alive. We have a much better chance together than either of us have on our own. You might not trust me now, but maybe I can earn your trust, if you give me a chance. And, besides, how do I know I can trust you? After all, you're the one who damn near choked me to death!"

Sonya said, "Yeah, well, okay, sorry about that. But I just wasn't gonna take any chances."

Raphael said, "I get it. But, believe me, I don't mean you any harm. I've seen too many people hurting other people, and I don't want to see that anymore. That's why I'm trying to get the hell away from all of this. I just want to get to some place where I can live my life in peace."

Sonya said, "That's what I want, too." Then she asked, "Do you have any family?"

He replied, "My family were all murdered by a gang. That's when, being as young and dumb as I was, I thought if I joined a rival gang, I could one day get revenge for my family. Man, how stupid is that? How about you? Do you have any family?"

She said, "I have my mom, and a little brother, and a little sister. But I had to leave them all behind because I had made some really stupid choices myself. I worry about them, all of the time."

Raphael said, "Sounds like our stories aren't that much different, except you can still have hope that your family is okay. I really hope they are. Maybe someday you will be able to reunite with them."

"That's really all I want," she said.

Raphael said, "First, we gotta get you out of here in one piece. Whaddya say? Will you let me help you?"

Sonya said, "Okay, but know this. I will be keeping one eye on you at all times. One false move, and-"

"Okay, okay, I get it," he said.

So, after talking for a little while longer, they settled in for some rest on opposite sides of the room. Raphael had shared with Sonya some food from his pack, which she quickly devoured, since she hadn't eaten anything all day. He had something to eat, as well, and before long, they had both fallen fast asleep. When they woke up, it was nearly dark outside. Now, they were about to begin their journey together.

They carefully and quietly snuck through the nights together, slowly inching their way closer and closer to anywhere but where they were now. They spent the days hiding together and watching each other's backs, and Sonya even began sharing with Raphael her story, little by little.

They had a long road ahead which gave them a lot of time to talk. They both began to understand just how much they had in common and cautiously became friends and earned each other's trust and respect. They were both equally stealthy and knowledgeable about how to pick good spots to hide out. They made a great team and both had the same goal. He never tried to make it anything more than a friend helping a friend. And she was always willing to make it very clear that it was going to stay that way. She eventually shared enough that he understood exactly why that was. She had been through more than anyone should be put through. Besides, he wasn't over losing the friend, who was obviously more than a friend to him, even if he never actually said it. So, they were on the same page.

Raphael had seen many things. He was always sharing tales of these things with Sonya.

One day while they were hiding out and talking, he said, "Ya know, we have always way underestimated dogs. They understand situations very well. Better than most people think. This one time, I had an injury that needed a few days to heal. So, I found a safe spot to hide out, on an upper floor of an abandoned apartment building. From there, I had a good view of the streets below, in all directions. This guy was walking with his dog and all of a sudden, another dude jumped out at him and shot him dead just to rob him for a watch worth twenty bucks at most. His dog stayed at his side like he was grieving the loss of his master. Another dog that had seen the whole thing happen befriended the orphaned dog and they eventually left together. A couple days later, these two dogs saw someone about to shoot at another person with a dog at their side and they viciously mauled and killed the attacker. They saw the person being attacked as a friend and would have defended that person to the death. People started to realize the significance of this and it became very common for people to travel with one or more dogs at their side as faithful companions and defenders. People who would have never shared their life with a dog before now valued dogs greatly. The bad guys even tried, sometimes, to kill people, to take their dogs once they realized how valuable a dog could be. But they would soon find out the hard way that it is futile and downright dangerous, because dogs will not change alliances so easily. They will die trying to protect their person. How many people do you know that will do that?"

Sonya said, "Aw, c'mon, you just made that up."

He said, "Nope, no way. It's absolutely true. I saw it with my own eyes."

Raphael told her another story of how, this one time, a guy had asked to buy a gun from him. Raphael said to Sonya, "He said that he had lots of money. You should have seen his face when I said, 'Oh, lots of money?' He said, 'Yeah.' I said, 'Hundred dollar bills?' He said, 'Yeah.' I said, 'Well, then you can feel really rich someday when you have no toilet paper and you use them to wipe your ass!'"

Sonya couldn't stop laughing about that story. But when she finally gathered herself, she said, "You have a gun?"

He replied, "Had one. Lost it a while back. We need to find some guns to protect ourselves."

Sonya said, "No guns for me."

He told her, "You may not like guns, and I get it, but

someday, you might just find yourself in a situation where a gun is an absolute necessity. It might be the only way for you to stay alive."

Raphael had many stories that he shared with Sonya. And everything he shared contained some sort of advice or some sort of lesson to help Sonya along the way. He turned every situation into a learning opportunity for her. You could say that he had become a mentor for her.

One night, while sneaking through a building, Sonya happened across some canned goods. "Look," she said, "This is great," and she began hastily stuffing them into the mostly empty pack that they had recently found for her.

Raphael stopped her and said, "No, no good. Too heavy and too noisy." He handed her his can opener and told her, "Eat all you can, then put one can in your pack. One can is quiet. More than one is too much weight and too much chance of making noise at a really bad time." He explained to her that you made use of those kinds of finds on the spot and only put lighter, quieter supplies in your pack. Then, they both proceeded to gorge themselves on the canned fruit and vegetables, quietly giggling at themselves for what pigs they were being. They felt like a couple of kids stealing from the pantry.

Raphael had learned many things in his travels and gladly passed along all of that knowledge to Sonya. She had always been pretty good at taking care of herself but with what he was teaching her from his experiences, she was getting even better. It wasn't a one-way street, though. He also learned some things from her along the way. And together they felt like they had a very real chance of getting out alive. Much better than either of them alone. They were each helping the other. They were truly a team and neither had any plans to go their own way. They had made up their minds to stick together and to both make it to where they needed to be. It was never a verbal agreement. It didn't have to be. They both just knew.

In spite of her cautiousness and reluctance to trust anyone, Sonya, little by little, started to think of Raphael as a true friend. His daily stories about the adventures he had experienced were always interesting to her. Some brought a tear to her eye. Some made her laugh. They all allowed her to feel like she knew him a little better. And the more she got to know him, the more she liked him. She always looked forward to hearing the tales he told.

Raphael started to think of Sonya as the little sister he never had. She had made it perfectly clear that their relationship would never go beyond being platonic. He was okay with that. She was smart and tough as nails. He knew that she was capable of taking care of herself, but still, he couldn't resist the need he felt to protect her.

# CHAPTER FIVE

## SONYA, MEET RAPHAEL

Although they had been traveling together for a while, now, Sonya still wanted to know more about Raphael. She wanted to know more about him as a person. But she had shared very little about herself to him, so she wasn't going to press him for information about himself. She figured he would share what he wanted to share in his own time.

One day while they were resting in one of their hiding spots along the way, Raphael was about two seconds from a deep sleep. She thought it might be time to let him know her name.

And, besides, if she shared a little something, maybe he would too.

She whispered, "Sonya."

He mumbled, "Huh, what?"

She said, "My name, it's Sonya."

He said, "Well, that is a much better name than 'Hey you'". He chuckled and began, again, to fall asleep.

Sonya asked, "What was her name?"

He said, "Huh, what, who?"

"The friend you went back to try to save," she said.

"Her name was Zola," he replied. He could see that she wasn't going to let him go to sleep.

She asked, “Were you two close?”

To which he replied, “Closer than I have ever been to anyone. We had each other’s backs, ya know? She saved my life more than once. And we would keep each other warm at night. She was the very best friend I have ever had. I loved her and she loved me. She was fierce, like you, but then she also had a very sweet side, not like you!” He laughed.

She kicked him in the leg and then laughed with him. “Yeah, and don’t you forget it!” she said. Sonya then said, “She sounds like a pretty special girl.”

He said, “None better. I would have given my life for her and she would have done the same for me. I really miss her.” His eyes were welling up with tears.

Sonya said, “You have my deepest sympathy. I’m truly sorry that you lost your friend.” With that, she figured it would be best to let him get some sleep and she should get some sleep, as well. She almost felt bad for making him revisit the pain of his loss. But she did get to see a little more of what he was all about. And she believed, even more, that he was a pretty good person.

Sonya and Raphael are doing well, so far. They have managed to stay out of sight. The progress has been slow, but is gradually getting a little better. They have escaped a few close calls when bad guys were near, just by remaining careful and quiet and being ever vigilant about their surroundings. They know that the further they go, the less trouble they should run into, but they know they can’t afford to get complacent. They have been fortunate enough to pick up supplies along the way. Even if a place has been thoroughly looted, you never know what could have been overlooked and left behind. Raphael has even managed to find a gun and some ammunition next to the body of someone less fortunate. Knowing Sonya's feelings towards guns, he quietly put it away in his pack. He hopes to never have to use it, but it is just a little insurance policy for some time when things go south. She has no idea he has it and he has yet to decide whether it would be better to tell her or just leave things as they are.

During another of their hideout conversations, Raphael stated that he just couldn't stop thinking about Zola. Sonya said that she hadn't brought the subject up again because she saw how much pain there was the last time they had talked about her. "But," she said, "if you feel like talking, I am willing to listen. That is what friends are for, right?"

"Friends?" he asked. "You were 'Hey You' a few days ago, and now we're friends?"

"Yeah, dummy, we're friends now. We've been spending a lot of time together and I'm starting to feel like I know you. And you seem like a pretty good person - for a guy, that is!"

This time, it was his turn to kick her in the leg as he smiled a little.

They had been eating some of the food that they had in their packs. Sometimes, they would trade back and forth like kids at a school lunch table. Raphael said, "Let me see if I can find something good enough in here that you'll trade me for one of those candy bars you have." He reached into his pack and way at the bottom he happened across something that he had forgotten was even in there. It was a little packet of dog treats. He said, "Man, Zola loved these things."

Sonya said, "Yuck! Are you kidding? You know those are dog treats, right?"

He said, "They're actually not half bad. Do you know that quality control for dog food is more closely monitored than some of the stuff made for people?"

She said, "Yeah, okay, great, but they are still dog treats. GROSS!"

He said, "Well, they're definitely not gross if you happen to be a dog."

Sonya took a long pause. "No way!" she thought to herself. She couldn't believe what she had just found out. She said, "You mean to tell me that the friend you came back for was a dog?"

He said, "Yeah, does that matter? She did more for me than any human ever did. She was my best friend. She was my Guardian Angel. A friend is a friend."

"Wow," she said. "Why didn't you tell me that before?"

Raphael replied, "You didn't ask. And I didn't think it mattered. Why? Were you jealous before you knew that Zola was a dog?"

She kicked him in the leg again, rolled her eyes, and said, "Hardly." Then she said, "Zola must have been one hell of a special dog for you to risk your life to come back for her."

He replied, "She was the best. You should have seen her. She never barked. She somehow knew that since I was being quiet and sneaky, that she should do the same. When I slept, she would sleep only a few minutes at a time while keeping a lookout the rest of the time. If she sensed trouble, she wouldn't make a sound. She would just nudge me with her nose and look in the direction of the trouble. I never trained her to do any of the things that she knew how to do. My best guess is that before I ended up with her, she must have been a police dog, or maybe a military dog. But even that wouldn't explain how she knew how to act in some of the situations we found ourselves in. She was special, alright. One of the times I told you about when she saved my…"

He was interrupted by Sonya saying, "You mean when I thought she was a human?"

He went on, "Yeah, one of those times. Anyway, she would normally walk right beside me or sometimes in front, but this time she was a couple steps behind me. This dude with a gun came around a corner in this dark hallway. He raised his gun to shoot me and in a single leap, Zola completely cleared me and hit him right in the face like one big muscle with teeth! He didn't know what the hell hit him. His shot missed both of us and the gun went flying. While Zola continued to use him for a chew toy, I retrieved the gun and we got the hell out of there."

Sonya asked, "So, how did you and Zola end up together?"

Raphael replied, "Remember the dog that I told you about, who had become a friend to the dog whose master had been shot? That was her. I have no idea what ever became of that other dog, but I found her wandering by herself one day and I recognized her right away. I offered her some food and gave her a little attention and that was it. She just stayed right by my side from that day on. She had no tags, so I had no idea what her name was. I wanted a unique name for her and came up with Zola. I guess she was okay with the name because she started responding to it right away."

Sonya said, with a wink, "Sounds like love at first sight, for both of you."

"You could say that, I guess," he said.

Raphael told Sonya of many more occasions when Zola had saved his life and about the amazing things she could do. He said, "Then, there was this one time, we were hiding in an old looted department store. I had fallen asleep with Zola right beside me. For some reason, I woke up and she was nowhere to be seen. I was really worried for her. I got up and slowly started searching, aisle by aisle, for her. I got about six aisles over, looked down the aisle, and there she was, sitting on top of what was left of this guy, holding his gun in her mouth. She had mauled the hell out of this guy, and did it so quietly that I never even woke up. When she saw me, she walked up to me and gently set the gun at my feet. Then she looked up at me as if to say, 'Look what I just did!'"

Sonya asked, "How could she have done all of that without you hearing a commotion?"

"I'll never know," he said. Raphael went on, "So, you see, yeah, she was something super special."

Then, Sonya asked, "So what happened? Sounds like you two were inseparable. How did you end up apart?"

He replied, "She would always do what she needed to do to protect me. But as soon as she had taken down the threat, she would come right back, stand at my side, and look up at me with the most gentle eyes you've ever seen. I never could figure out how she could flip the switch so fast like that. One minute, she was a snarling, growling, foaming at the mouth attack dog. The next minute, she was a loving, cuddly, treat-begging puppy dog. Anyway, this one time was different.

She had disarmed this guy but he somehow got away. His buddies drove by and he jumped into the truck while it was still moving. The threat was no longer there, but for some reason, she chased after them. I tried to call her back, but she just kept going. The only thing I can figure is that she recognized this guy as someone she had maybe encountered before and had a score to settle with him. It was totally unlike anything she had ever done before. I didn't dare hang around, knowing that someone had to have heard all the commotion. I had to get out of there. I knew the spot and planned to return after things had a chance to calm down. I had always hoped that she would know I would be back for her and to keep an eye out for me. And she did. I found her right where we had last been together. She had been shot and was lying there in a pool of blood. She was barely breathing when I got to her. She died in my arms just a few minutes later. It was like she had only hung on to say goodbye."

Raphael began sobbing. By this time, Sonya was crying too. She put her arms around him as they cried together. Raphael said, "Don't get any ideas, right?"

She said, "Exactly."

Now they were laughing and crying at the same time. She said, "Pass those dog treats, will ya?" They both started eating the dog treats. Sonya held one up and said, "To Zola!"

Raphael held one up and said, "To Zola!"

Sonya said, "You're right. These actually aren't half bad."

Sonya learned a lot about Raphael that day. She now knew for sure that he had the kindest, most gentle soul of anyone she had ever met. And she knew that he would do absolutely anything for a friend. He would be loyal to the death just like Zola had been. She knew that she could count on him to have her back, no matter what. And she knew that she would always have his back the same way. There was no denying the fact that both of them felt the same way. They were a team. Neither of them had ever had a friendship that ran this deep before. And it always stayed that way for both of them. It was like a brother/sister relationship, only even stronger, if that's possible.

Feeling more and more like Raphael was turning out to be a pretty good friend, she decided to share a little more of her story with him. She said, "I really need to get away from here, but I feel so guilty because I had to leave my mom and my little sister and brother behind. I knew the gang would be coming after me, so it wouldn't be safe for me to stay with them. It would also not be safe to try to have them come with me. I promised that I would go back for them, but I have no idea if I will be able to keep that promise. I just wish I knew if they were okay. What if I do go back, and find out that something bad has happened to them? How will I live with myself, then?"

Raphael said, "It sounds, to me, like you didn't have much of a choice. You can't beat yourself up about it. You did what you had to do, as difficult as it was. All you can do now is try to stay positive and hopeful that they will be okay. That will give you a reason to go on. Keep thinking about seeing them again, someday. That will give you something to fight for. I can't promise you that they will be okay, but you have to keep believing that they are. Never, ever give up, alright?"

"Alright," she said, "and, thanks. I really needed to hear that. I feel better, having you reassure me that I did the right thing, because it sure didn't feel like the right thing at the time."

Raphael said, "You did what you did out of love. It was what you believed would be best for your family's safety. When you do something out of love, it is always the right thing."

Any doubts that Sonya had previously had about Raphael had now evaporated. His stories, his encouraging words, and his devotion to a friend had all served to leave her with no doubt that he was a great human being.

# CHAPTER SIX

## ENEMY, MEET SONYA AND RAPHAEL

Sonya and Raphael continued to make slow but steady progress. They had made it out of the inner city and were now working their way through a mostly industrial area. Most of the really violent gang activity was now behind them, but not all. The area they were now in still held resources that the "super gangs" could make use of. So, there were always a few groups of gang members lurking around, checking the factories and warehouses for things they could use. For example, they would steal heavy equipment for use in everything from destroying government buildings to prevent any remaining government officials from having a place to work, to barricading streets and alleys to slow down anyone who might try to launch any sort of assault on them. This equipment was also used to destroy law enforcement facilities and to facilitate prison breaks. There were many other items in these areas that would be of use to them, so they always had a presence here. So, Sonya and Raphael could not let their guard down for even a second.

For the last several days, Sonya had noticed that Raphael would spend a few minutes each day, before getting some rest, drawing and scribbling something in a notebook that he kept in his pack.

She asked him, "What is that you're doing in that book of

yours?"

Raphael replied, "As I made my way out last time, I made a sort of map of where I went and kept notes of important things along the way. On my way back in, to... well, you know, "I used it to find my way and stay away from trouble spots. Now, things keep changing, but most of what I have here still shows the safest route, that I know of, between where we were and where we need to go. I am making a copy of it for you, just in case we get separated or in case something happens to me. I care about you and I want you to get out safely, even if I am not there to help you."

Sonya said, "Nothing is going to happen to you. We are being careful and we will get out of here, together."

"I hope you're right", he said, "but just in case, I want you to be able to find your way. This map will help you do that if it becomes necessary. And I almost have your copy done." He did a little more drawing and writing, then handed it to her.

Sonya said, "I really appreciate the way you've been looking out for me. Thanks for this map. But I don't plan on ever needing it."

Raphael said, "You're welcome. You are like a sister to me. Keep that somewhere safe in your pack. I, also, hope you never need it! But I will feel much better knowing you have it, just in case. Now let's try to get some rest."

She said, with a wink, "Nighty, night, Brother."

As they were both nodding off to sleep, they were suddenly greeted with a metallic clank, like a tool being dropped on the floor. Someone else had invaded their hiding spot! They always kept a little distance between themselves when they slept, so as not to both be spotted at the same time by anyone who might be trying to harm them, but still remained within sight of one another, all in case of a situation just like this. All it took for them to know what the other was thinking was eye contact. They could almost read each other's minds. They had discussed what they would do if scenarios like this came about. They had come up with a few basic hand signals to use while dealing with such situations, as well. Their ability to work as a team, against a common foe, hadn't been tested in real life, but was well rehearsed through all of the discussions they had had. So, with a meeting of their eyes and a couple of simple head nods and gestures, Raphael snuck in one direction while Sonya crept in another. As always, their hiding spot had been carefully selected to have more than one way out, and with as few ways for trouble to come from as possible. Raphael, always concerned for Sonya's safety, insisted upon being the one to head towards any perceived threat, while she was supposed to head away from that threat, while staying close enough to provide backup, if needed. But things don't always go according to plan. The intruder took an unexpected turn and Sonya ended up directly in the intruder's path. From where she was hiding, she could see the gang tattoos on this dude and could also see the gun in his waistband. In a couple more steps, this guy would be right on top of Sonya, and her hiding spot would no longer offer any cover. Raphael had reached a spot where he could see what was unfolding, and quickly realized that all he could do to help her was to create a distraction and hope that she would be able to take advantage of the opportunity to do whatever she had to do to protect herself until he could get there to help. He considered, for a second, that it might be time to use the gun he had stashed in his pack, but the last thing he wanted was to draw the attention of any other bad guys that might hear the shot. So, he picked up a piece of broken brick and threw it at the intruder, striking him in the back.

As the intruder spun around to see what had hit him, drawing his gun, at the same time Sonya put into practice what she had learned from her father and the Martial Arts classes she had taken all those years ago. In one seamless and lightning-fast motion, she somehow simultaneously kicked the gun out of his hand, and landed a blow with the other foot that put him face down on the floor. This all occurred before she ever made contact with the floor again herself. When she did touch down, her momentum put her elbow, forcefully, into the back of his neck. The man was disarmed and unconscious within about five seconds. Raphael hadn't even had time to make a move to assist her. He simply watched, in utter amazement, what Sonya had just done. When he got to where she was, he was speechless. He just stared at her with his eyes wide and his chin nearly touching his chest.

She shrugged her shoulders and said, "What?"

He said, "I've never seen anything like that in my life!"

It wasn't safe to go looking for a new hideout, since it was daylight out, so they needed to make sure this guy couldn't do any harm to them when he woke up. They tied him up, very securely, and gagged him so he couldn't call out for help. Then they took him to another room, and locked him up in a closet. Then they returned to their hiding spots and tried to get some rest. But Raphael wasn't going to take any chances. Once Sonya had fallen asleep, he went back and snapped the neck of the intruder to make sure he wouldn't be causing them any more problems. He didn't want Sonya to see this. He wasn't exactly sure why. It just didn't feel right to do such a thing in front of her. He was feeling ever more protective of her. She was tough, but he didn't want to expose her to any more violence than he had to. He just knew that under that tough as nails exterior was still a sweet girl on the inside. He wanted to protect as much of her innocence as possible.

A few nights later, they were carefully making their way through a railyard, using parked train cars for cover. They stopped occasionally to look in all directions, under the cars to make sure no one else was around. In addition to looking, they would also listen, carefully, for any sound that may mean they weren't there alone. They had made it about halfway through a long stretch of two rows of train cars with not much of anything else for cover on either side. They needed to make it to the end and find a place to hide out, since morning was quickly approaching. There were no places to hide behind them, but there were some buildings up ahead which were used for performing maintenance on locomotives. They needed to get there before it got light.

When they had made it to about one hundred yards from where the two rows of cars ended, a figure appeared between the last two cars. Sonya and Raphael could see that this individual was carrying a rifle and was heading in their direction. They knew that there was nowhere to go but forward. They also knew that there was not enough cover to sneak past this person. They knew that they would have to take this guy out if they were to make it to their destination. So, in typical fashion, a couple of gestures, glances, and head nods were all that was necessary for them to know what the plan was. Raphael rolled under a car on one side and made his way to the coupler connecting two cars and climbed up onto it, while Sonya, moving like a cat, climbed silently up the ladder on the end of one of the cars, on the other side. She got on top of the car and slid, quietly, on her belly, in the direction of the threat. This would put her one train car length behind the intruder as he reached Raphael's position. They both just silently waited while the dude kept heading in their direction, and eventually passed where Sonya was. She had picked up a rock from the railbed and just inches before the intruder reached where Raphael was, she threw it at the car across from where she was. As he spun around to see what the noise was, Raphael, swinging around the ladder on the end of the train car, hit the guy with a drop kick, from behind, that put him down hard. In a second, Raphael was on top of him, choking him with his own rifle. By the time Sonya had climbed down to offer assistance, the guy was dead.

Sonya gave Raphael a look, much like the look on Raphael's face a few nights earlier when she had taken down a bad guy, and stood there, speechless.

Raphael shrugged his shoulders and said, "What?" Sonya said, "I had no idea you had moves like that!"

"Me neither!" he said. "I guess you just do what ya gotta do, sometimes."

Sonya said, "Yeah, I guess so. What do you say we find a place to get some rest? I think we earned it!"

Raphael said, "Sounds like a great idea. Let's go."

So, they continued on to the buildings up ahead. When they got there, they carefully and thoroughly looked around to make sure there weren't any other bad guys around, and once satisfied that they had the place to themselves, they found their hiding spots for the day. They were snacking on some of their supplies from their packs and talking, like they always did, before settling in for some sleep.

Sonya said, "We make a pretty good team, don't you think?" Raphael said, "Yeah, we sure do."

Sonya said, "Those were some pretty impressive moves, out there."

Raphael said, "Not half as impressive as what you did a few days ago. Where did you learn to do that?"

Not wanting to give any credit to her father, she said, "I took some Martial Arts classes when I was younger and had a few other people teach me some moves along the way. Where did you learn your moves?"

He said, "Gang fighting taught me how to handle myself, mostly. Other than that, movies."

"Movies?" she asked.

"Yeah, I watched a lot of Jackie Chan movies, and Chuck Norris, and Bruce Lee. I loved that stuff when I was a kid. I would watch them over and over again and then I would imitate what they did. I practiced those moves until I could do them almost as well as those guys did. My best friend, back then, watched that stuff with me and we practiced together. We gave each other lots of bruises and bloody noses, but we eventually got pretty good at it."

Sonya said, "I would have never believed you could learn to do those things from movies, but it looks like it worked for you."

Raphael then said, "Well, I don't know about you, but I am beat. Let's get some rest, huh?"

She said, "Sounds good. I'm pretty tired, myself."

As they settled in for some much-needed sleep, they had no idea how little rest they were going to get. As always, they had carefully selected their hiding spots. This building had an upper level, around the perimeter of the building, with limited access points, which meant fewer directions from which trouble could come. There was an elevated catwalk connecting the two sides of the upper level. Sonya had settled in on one side, and Raphael on the other. They had a clear line of sight between them, across the catwalk.

Less than an hour after they had dozed off, they were awakened by the squeaking of a door being opened. As they both looked down to see what or who had caused the sound, Raphael couldn't see anything, but Sonya could clearly see two men entering through the door directly below Raphael's location. They were carrying guns and were obviously gang members, probably looking for tools or other useful items to steal. Sonya and Raphael both realized that these two would eventually be heading up to where they were. It would be better to take them out before that happened, while the element of surprise was still on their side. It was going to be tricky, to say the least, with two intruders to deal with. Sonya and Raphael would have to time their movements for when they were out of the line of sight of both of the men below. When the opportunity presented itself, Sonya silently made her way to a spot near the center of the catwalk that had a section of solid wall on the railings on both sides. With their nearly psychic way of communicating, Sonya and Raphael were keeping one another aware of where the men were at all times. One of the men was looking around along the outer wall of the room which made it possible for Raphael to keep directly above him, with the help of Sonya's glances and gestures. She couldn't see what the other man was doing, but Raphael indicated to her that he was about to cross the room and be under her location soon. At the very second that he passed under where Sonya was, both Sonya and Raphael jumped the railings and launched simultaneous attacks from above on the two men. The heavy wrenches that Sonya and Raphael had armed themselves with landed deadly blows to the skulls of the two men at the exact same time. Neither of them ever knew what hit them.

Raphael said, “Sonya and Raphael - four, bad guys - zero.”

Sonya said, “Like I said before, we make a helluva team!”

After a few high fives, and a celebratory hug, they went back to their hiding spots and finally got some much needed and hard-earned rest. As they were drifting off to sleep, they were both thinking about how they have proven themselves to be a force to be reckoned with. At the same time, they were both hoping that they would not have to prove themselves many more times. As fortunate as they had been, up to now, there were no guarantees that things would always turn out so well. They have managed to take out single enemies a couple times. They have, just now, even managed to take down two bad guys at once. What if, at some point, there is a whole group of foes bearing down on them at once? That might not end so well. They needed to be even more careful to avoid that kind of situation.

# CHAPTER SEVEN

## SONYA AND RAPHAEL, MEET A FRIEND

Late in the afternoon, Sonya and Raphael woke up and were having something to eat. This was their time to talk and plan their next night's movements.

Sonya asked, "So, where are we heading, next?"

Raphael said, "Maybe we should see how good of a job I did on that map. You should see if you can tell me where we are going next. You know, just for practice."

Sonya said, "Okay." She dug her copy of the map out of her pack. After looking at it for a few minutes, she said, "It looks like we go this way," pointing to the map, "and once we are out of this trainyard, that would be a suburb, right?"

Raphael said, "That's exactly right."

"So, we should have an easier time there, right?" she asked.

"A little, maybe, but not much better until we get way out to here," he said, pointing to the map.

Where he was pointing was a long way from where they were now. "When I went through this area before, there were only a few bad guys out this far. Just a little beyond that, there were still a few good people fighting to hold the gangs back, but they were already losing ground. I'm sure the bad guys have pushed them even farther back, by now. We will still need to be on point."

She then asked, "So, who are these 'good people' that you mentioned?"

He replied, "Some are just residents of the area, who have weapons, and are able and willing to use them. Some are former law enforcement. Some are military people. They are pretty special people, when you think about it. They are outnumbered and outgunned, but they are not willing to give up, fighting against the thugs who are taking over their communities."

Then Sonya asked, "What are these circles, with the letter 'R' inside them, with arrows pointing towards the very edges of the map?"

Raphael replied, "The 'R' stands for rescue. I talked to some of the people who are going in with small groups to get as many people out of the city as they can before the bad guys kill them. They told me, roughly, what direction they were taking these folks, to get them somewhere safer. I marked these on the map, if for no other reason, to know what direction some of these safer areas were. I did it so that if and when I got out farther than where I had been before, I would have an idea where it would be best to go."

Sonya asked, "Do you think it's possible that my mom and my little brother and sister could have been helped to one of those places?"

He said, "I wouldn't get your hopes up too much, but sure, it's possible."

She said, "Well, I'm so glad you put that on the map. If I make it out of here, I will look for as long as it takes to see if my family made it out. Thank you."

Raphael said, "If we make it that far, I will help you. I

have nothing else to do."

Sonya said, "Ya know, you are the best friend I have ever had. You've helped me so much in the short time we've known each other. Do you think we could stay friends after we get through all of this?"

Raphael replied, "Like I said before, I don't have anywhere else to go or anyone to get back to out there, so, yeah, I would really like it if we could stay friends, once we get out of here. No matter where we go, there will eventually be situations where it would be good to have someone who has your back, and someone you can trust. I should be thanking you, too, because you have been the best friend I have ever had, as well - human friend, that is. So, what do you say? Teammates forever?"

"You got it!" she replied.

With that, they gathered up their supplies and arranged them back into their packs. It would be dark soon, and that would mean that it was time to spend yet another night sneaking through the darkness to get closer to a safer place than what they were leaving. That was always the goal. Complete safety was never a realistic goal, but someplace safer than where they were was always within reach. That is what gave them the strength to keep going.

Seeing that Sonya seemed to have a pretty good grasp on where to go from looking at the map, Raphael said, "Okay, you've got point."

Sonya took one last look at the map and then put it back in her pack. She said, "Alright, just a few more minutes until dark, then we will head that way."

"I'm with you, Sister," Raphael said.

As darkness fell, they began to make their way out of the

railyard which had provided much more adventure than they had bargained for. They would be happy to have no more of that sort of adventure.

Things were quiet, and there was no sign of anyone around, so they were able to make quick work of getting to the property fence at the edge of the railyard. They found a hole in the fence to crawl through, and then proceeded across an open field. Before long, they were moving into the suburban area which Sonya had picked out on the map.

Raphael said, "I'm impressed. You followed the route exactly as I drew it on the map, even though you haven't looked at it again since we started out." Then he said, with a wink, "Not bad ...for a girl!"

Sonya gently elbowed him in the ribs, winked back at him, and said, "Thanks, Brother."

Raphael then said, "Just remember, things could have changed since I was here before, so we need to be super careful. Now that we are in a residential area, there are more places for bad guys to be where they might be hard for us to spot. Trouble could come around any corner at any time. And there is a very good chance that we will be too close for comfort by the time we can see them. So, we need to slow way down, peek around every corner, stay absolutely silent, and really listen closely, at all times. It may seem like it is taking forever to get anywhere, but we have to be patient. We made it this far. We sure don't want to get careless now and have everything we've accomplished be for nothing. The same things that make it hard for us to spot them also makes it harder for them to spot us. We need to make use of all the cover we can to stay out of sight. Houses, garages, garden sheds, hedges, bushes, cars, whatever is available should all be used to keep our movements concealed. Stay in the shadows as much as possible."

Sonya said, "Okay, I understand. But I am so ready to be away from all of this that I might get moving too fast. If I do, you may need to remind me, okay?"

He said, "You got it." Then he gave her a smile and a thumbs up.

Sonya then asked, "What sorts of things should we be watching for? I mean, like how will we be able to tell if things have changed since you were here?"

Raphael replied, "Well, one thing already worries me a little. It's not that late. Do you see any lights on in these houses around us?"

"No, why do you think that is?" she asked.

He said, "That tells me one of two things. Either these folks have already evacuated while they had the chance, before the gangs got here, or the gangs have already been here and there is no one left here, because they have already been killed or they were forced to flee. If the first is true, the gangs could still be behind us, which would be better than if the second is true, in which case, the gangs would be ahead of us. As we move forward, we will get a better idea of the situation.

When we get around some of the stores and local businesses, we will be able to see whether they have been looted or not. That will give us a good idea as to who's been around."

"Got it. That makes sense," Sonya said.

With that, they started to inch their way through the suburb, carefully watching and listening for any signs of activity, friendly or not friendly. They passed through backyards of homes along the way as much of the time as possible. This offered them as much cover as could be found anywhere and also provided access to places to hide quickly, should the need arise. Whether there was a garden shed to get into, or just some shrubs or bushes to duck into, it was much better than getting caught, out in the open, on the street. And the backyards were usually relatively dark, which greatly aided in concealing their movements. It was slow going, since there were many fences to climb over or crawl under, as well as hedges and other obstacles to work their way past, but the extra time it took was well worth it for the added safety it provided them.

They had made their way through a couple dozen backyards, and were starting to look for a place to hide for the upcoming day, because it would be morning soon. Sonya and Raphael found themselves in a yard with a garden shed in the back corner, about fifty yards from the house. There were no lights on in the house, so either no one was in the house, or they were just not up and about, yet. In fact, the entire neighborhood was dark.

Sonya asked, "Do you think anyone is home here?"

Raphael said, "It doesn't look like anyone is home in the whole neighborhood, but let's proceed with the same kind of caution as we would if we knew somebody was in the house, just in case."

Sonya said, "Roger that." Even though she had done everything in her power to completely remove any sign of her father from her life, sometimes little things from the past still surfaced without her even being conscious of it. That little phrase was something Sonya and her father used to say to one another all the time. It is a phrase that the Seals use frequently, and it rubbed off on Sonya when she was a little girl.

Raphael asked, “Roger that? Never heard you say that before. Did you spend a lot of time around someone who was in the military, or something?”

Sonya had never told Raphael anything about her father, because it was a subject she didn’t like talking about. She didn’t want to talk about him now, either. She would prefer to leave him in her past and do her best to just forget about him, because of how bad things had been leading up to their parting of ways. So, she simply said, “Yeah, uh, I had an uncle who was in the Navy. He used to say that a lot. I used to say it back to him when I was little. That was a long time ago, so I’m not sure why I said it just now. Weird, huh? So, what do you say we take a look at that shed over there? It’ll be light soon.”

Raphael said, “Yeah, okay, let’s have a look.” Raphael couldn’t help but notice how quickly Sonya had changed the subject. He had his suspicions that there was something she didn’t want to talk about.

There was just something about the way she spoke so rapidly, all the while avoiding eye contact. But he decided it best to leave well enough alone. If it was something she ever wanted to share, she would do it in her own time.

They went to the shed to see what kind of a hideout it would be for the day ahead. They decided that it would do nicely. It had a walk-in door on the side facing the house, and a small overhead door on the opposite end. There was a tall wooden fence around the yard, not far from the overhead door, and Raphael knew that the safest place for Sonya would be just inside the overhead door. He lifted the door open, just enough that Sonya could roll underneath if necessary.

Raphael said, “You can make a spot for yourself right over there, just inside that door. I will be just inside the other door. That gives us two ways out in case we need to leave quickly. Things seem pretty quiet around here, so I don’t expect any surprises, but we can’t be too careful.”

“Okay,” Sonya said.

They had a little to eat and talked for a while, like they did every morning. Then they went to the places they had made for themselves to get some rest. Not long after they had gotten settled, and before they had even come close to going to sleep, there was the sound of the door near Raphael swinging open and the distinctive sound of the hammer of a revolver being cocked. Sonya immediately rolled under the door and quietly started to sneak around the shed. At the exact same time, Raphael was being asked, “Who are you and what the hell are you doing in my yard?”

Raphael said, “I’m not here to take anything or to do you any harm.” He chose his words carefully, so as not to reveal that there was anyone else there but him. He could see how much the gun pointed at him was shaking and he could tell that this was simply a homeowner defending himself and his property. He added, “I just needed a place to rest for a few hours.”

By this time, Sonya had managed to position herself behind the man pointing the gun at Raphael.

Raphael could see that she was like a coiled spring, ready to unleash a disarming blow on the man. He didn’t think the man was likely to shoot, as long as he kept calm. He gave a barely perceptible nod to Sonya, which along with his eyes and expression, told her not to attack the man. So, she backed away, but not too far.

Raphael said, "Please, sir, just let us leave peacefully. Meet my friend, Sonya, behind you there. We truly don't want any trouble. We're just passing through. We just needed some rest and a place to stay out of sight until dark."

The man said, "Until dark? Who are you running from?"

Raphael said, "Things have gotten really bad where we came from. The gangs have taken over and we are just trying to get away from the city, alive. My name is Raphael, by the way."

The man replied, "I'm Frank."

Sonya said, "Pleased to meet you, Frank. My friend is telling you the truth. We mean you no harm."

Frank said, "Okay. I believe you. If you were going to hurt me, you could have done that already. Sonya, Raphael, why don't you come inside? My wife passed away several years ago, so I have the place all to myself. You can rest, and if you would like, I can make some coffee, or something to eat. Most of the trouble has already passed through here, but we would still be much safer inside."

Raphael said, "Thank you, so much. You are very kind."

Sonya said, "I'm so sorry about your wife's passing. We truly appreciate this."

They all went into Frank's house and he made them something to eat. Sonya and Raphael were so tired they could barely keep their eyes open. They both thanked Frank for the first home cooked meal they had eaten in weeks. Frank, seeing how tired they were, put out some blankets on the couches in his living room and told them to get some rest and make themselves at home.

Frank said, "You two, get some rest. I used to work the

night shift, so I know how you feel. You're kinda doing the same thing, it sounds like." He pulled down all of the shades to darken the room and before he had even finished doing that, his guests were sound asleep. They hadn't had a soft, warm, comfortable place to sleep for a long time and it was the best sleep they had experienced since what felt like forever.

In the late afternoon, Sonya and Raphael were awakened by the aroma of coffee brewing, bacon and eggs frying, and pancakes cooking. These were smells which neither of them had smelled for a very long time. Frank came in to wake them for breakfast, but they were already sitting on the edges of their couches.

Frank said, "It looks like you two are ready for a good breakfast. C'mon into the kitchen and have a seat."

Sonya said, "Coffee! Do you know how much I've missed having coffee?"

Frank said, "I made a great big pot, so you're welcome to all you want."

Raphael asked, "With all that has happened, how is it that you have food like this? I mean, it's not like you can just go to a store and get it any more, right?"

Frank replied, "It wasn't all that long ago that the trouble started around here. I had stocked up on supplies before it all happened. I also have some relatives who have a farm about thirty miles from here. They would occasionally come and give me fresh eggs, vegetables from their garden, and whatever else they had that they thought I could use. I'm not sure if they will be able to do that any more. Besides that, when my wife was still alive, she insisted that we should have all sorts of non-perishable items around in case of some sort of disaster. I thought she was crazy, at the time, for having such a stockpile of such things. But now I'm thankful that she was such a prepper. There are shelves in the basement, just loaded with canned goods, MREs, coffee, and just about everything you can think of that has a long shelf life. I could literally survive for years on that stuff."

Sonya asked, "So, how did you not get robbed or killed by the gangs?"

Frank said, "Mostly just lucky, I guess. Not everyone around here was so lucky. I just kept my head down, my lights off, and kept quiet inside. Somehow, I was just fortunate that they passed by without ever stopping at my house."

Sonya said, "I'm glad you were so lucky. You are a very good person and you don't deserve to be hurt like so many others have."

Raphael said, "Frank, I don't know how we can thank you enough for your kindness. It will be dark in a couple hours. Then we will be on our way."

Frank said, "I know you two are eager to get going. But you're obviously beat from what you've been through so far. You could use more rest before you move on. Won't you please stay one more day? I insist. I'm enjoying the company, anyway. Another day of rest and a little more real food in your bellies will do you good."

Sonya said, "Oh, I don't know. I mean, you've already done so much for us. We don't want to impose."

Raphael said, "Yeah, we should really get going."

Frank said, "Nonsense! You're not imposing at all. Please, stay one more day. Then you can be on your way. Don't hurt an old man's feelings."

Sonya and Raphael looked at each other and said, at the

same time, "Okay."

The three of them sat and talked for hours. Frank treated them like he had known them for years. They told him of some of the adventures they had experienced so far. He listened intently to everything they had to say.

Sonya asked, "So, what if the gangs come through here again? You may not be so lucky next time. Don't you think you should try to find somewhere safer?"

Frank replied, "This is my home. I'm an old man and I don't think I could handle the kind of traveling you two have been doing. I don't really know where else I would go, anyway. Besides, I don't know where I would be any safer than right here. Come with me. I want to show you something." As he led them down the stairs into the basement, he said, "Remember how I told you my wife was a prepper? Well, have a look at this."

At the opposite end of the basement, Frank grasped a shelving unit and as he pulled on it, a hidden door swung open. The shelving unit was attached to this door in such a way that it all blended in seamlessly with the wall, making it totally invisible. Frank entered and Sonya and Raphael followed.

Then, Frank pulled the door shut behind them and latched it securely. Frank could see that this seemed to be creeping out his guests. He told them not to worry and explained that it was just protocol to always have the door secured any time he entered. It would be pointless to have a hidden door if it didn't stay hidden at all times. Then he led the way down a long, narrow hallway. At the end of the hallway, they entered a room about the size of two school buses. There were a couple bunk beds, shelves loaded with bottled water and non-perishable food items, and all sorts of supplies. There were two shotguns, a rifle, and another hand gun, as well as a large amount of ammunition for all of the weapons on a rack near the bunk beds.

Sonya and Raphael looked around in utter amazement. Raphael said, "Looks like you are prepared for just about anything!"

Frank said, "I told you my wife was a prepper! A few years back, these backyard bunkers became a thing. There were several companies that sprang up solely to sell them to homeowners who wanted a secure place to ride out any sort of disaster that might happen. She saw something about it on TV, and her mind was made up. She just had to have one. So, here it is. And this ladder in the corner leads to a hidden hatch into the garden shed I found you in. I told her it felt like being in a submarine. I joked that it needed a periscope. I was only joking, for crying out loud. She thought that sounded like a great idea. So, guess what I had to do next. At her insistence, I had to build a periscope! Here, have a look."

As Sonya and Raphael took turns looking through the periscope, Frank explained how he had concealed it within the chimney pipe of the wood burning stove which sat in one corner of the garden shed. That chimney pipe also served to allow fresh air into the bunker.

Sonya said, "Ingenious!"

Frank said, "In hindsight, the periscope idea actually was a good idea. If I'm ever forced to take shelter down here, at least I can see when it looks safe to go back out. So, as you can see, I'm probably safer in my own home than anywhere else. You don't need to worry about old Frank."

Raphael said, “Yeah, it looks like you could survive almost anything. Pretty amazing.”

With that, they all left Frank’s bunker and went back to his house where they continued their conversation, which they were all thoroughly enjoying. Eventually, Sonya couldn’t keep her eyes open any longer and nodded off. Raphael and Frank talked for a while longer, but Frank could see that Raphael’s eyes were getting heavy, too.

Frank said, “Look at that. She’s sleeping like a baby. I told you that you two needed some more rest. If you’re heading out tonight, you should get some sleep, as well.”

Raphael said, “Yeah, I guess so. I just want to thank you again for being so kind to us.”

Frank said, “You’re very welcome. Now, get some rest, okay?”

Sonya and Raphael slept all through the day. They really did need this break, more than they knew. Once again, in the late afternoon, they were greeted by the irresistible aromas of coffee and the good, hot meal which Frank had prepared for them. When they walked into the kitchen, they saw that Frank had laid out some supplies for them on his counter to take with them. He told them that they were welcome to take all they wanted. The three of them sat down to a great meal, and enjoyed some more good company. When they had finished eating, they all realized that saying goodbye was going to be difficult. In just a couple of short days, they had become friends to a degree that usually takes years.

Raphael said, “Well, Frank, I guess this is it. I don’t know how we can thank you enough.”

Frank said, “You can thank me by making it safely to

wherever you are heading."

Raphael reached to shake Frank's hand and Frank reached right back. The man had the firmest handshake Raphael had ever felt.

Then Frank extended his hand to Sonya. Sonya went right past Frank's outstretched hand and wrapped her arms around Frank to give him a huge hug.

She said, with tears in her eyes, "You're a very sweet man. I wish only the best for you. Thank you so much for being such a great friend. You take care of yourself, okay?"

Frank said, "I will. You take care, too. I wish the best for you, as well."

Raphael said, "Well, Sonya, we better get going."

Frank asked, "So, where is it that you two are hoping to get to?"

Raphael replied, "I just want to get away from all of the violence. I just want to get to somewhere peaceful. Sonya has an even more important goal, though."

Frank asked, "Which is?"

Sonya said, "I had to leave my mom and my little brother and sister behind. I just have to find them. I've been so worried about them since I left."

Frank said, "I hope you find them. I wish you all the luck in the world."

With that, Sonya and Raphael walked out of Frank's back door, into the darkness. She was still wiping the tears from her eyes as they left.

She said, "What an awesome man. Why can't everyone be like that?"

Raphael said, "Yep. If everyone was like old Frank, there, the world would be a much better place, for sure."

They made good progress that night, and as morning approached, they nearly forgot that they needed to, once again, find some place to hide out for the next day. They had been spoiled by Frank's hospitality for the past two days. Now, they were on their own, again. When they had settled into a hiding spot, their entire conversation revolved around Frank and what a good friend he had been to them. They knew that they would never forget him.

# CHAPTER EIGHT

## SONYA, MEET PAIN

Another night was approaching and Sonya and Raphael were getting ready to continue their journey. As always, they were having something to eat, talking, and planning their route for the night ahead. Sonya said, “Those couple days of rest really did me some good. I feel more ready to go than I have in a long time. To be honest, I was getting pretty burned out.”

Raphael said, “Yeah, I hear ya. I was pretty beat myself. It felt good to take a break. It would have been pretty easy to just keep hanging out with old Frank back there.”

Sonya said, “What an awesome guy, huh? There aren’t many people who would have taken us in like that during good times. And there are even fewer, if any, who would do that the way things are now.”

“That’s for sure,” Raphael said. He continued, “He treated us like family, almost as if he was our father.”

Sonya, not wanting to compare Frank to the man she had lost all respect for, quickly changed the subject, saying, “Well, we better get moving, huh?”

Raphael said, “Yeah, I guess so.” Then he asked, “Can I ask you something?”

She said, “Sure.”

He said, “We’ve talked about everything under the sun. But I’ve noticed, on several occasions, now, that you’ve never said anything about your father. And just now, when I said Frank was kinda like a father, you couldn't change the subject fast enough. It's not the first time. Why is that?"

She replied, "Let's just say that he was once a good man, but then he changed into something totally different. Things didn't end well between us and I just don't like thinking about it. And I don't like talking about him."

Raphael said, "Okay, I won't bring it up again, but I just have one last thing to say. If he was a good man once, there's probably still a good man inside him. No matter what it was that tore you two apart, he still loves you. Fathers never stop loving their little girls. People screw up, sometimes. And, sometimes, things happen in our lives that make us say or do horrible things. Don't spend the rest of your life carrying around that anger towards your dad. It will eat you up inside. Okay, that's all I've got to say."

Sonya didn't say anything, but he could see from her expression that his point had been made. She was busily gathering her things and stuffing them into her pack. He was doing the same. When they both finished packing up, they left their hiding spot and headed out. Raphael glanced at Sonya and she looked back with a half-smile and a nod, as if to say that she understood what he had just said to her.

As they proceeded, they could see and hear that there was more activity ahead of them. There was the occasional sound of tires squealing, people shouting, and gunshots. They were both glad that they were well rested from the last few days. They were obviously going to need all their strength for what laid ahead.

Raphael said, "We're catching up to the bad guys, now. We

need to figure out where there might be gaps in the action. It's still too far away to really tell where those gaps might be. But when we get a little closer, we should be able to tell, by listening, what directions the most noise is coming from. Then, with a little luck, we can try to go through the quietest areas we can find. It's not going to be easy."

Sonya said, "I don't think we can afford to rush this. How about we try to get a little closer, like you were saying, and find a place to hide where we can just spend tomorrow watching and listening? Then, hopefully, we will be able to come up with a plan for tomorrow night."

Raphael said, "That sounds like a very smart idea to me. Maybe we can get there while there's still a few hours left before morning. That way, since there seems to be a lot going on right now, we can get a head start on our recon."

So, they carefully made their way through the darkness until they found a suitable place to hide.

They were now close enough to hear what directions the sounds were all coming from. They had been lucky enough to find a six-story office building, which they slowly and methodically entered and investigated, floor by floor, to make sure no one else was inside. Once they had determined they were alone in the building, they made their way to the roof. This would be the ideal spot to observe their surroundings from. There was only one way onto the roof, so it was about the safest place to be. It was also the highest building in the area, which made it a great vantage point to see in all directions. And pinpointing the directions of sounds was much easier from up here as well. They spent the next few hours just watching and listening, paying close attention to what areas seemed to have the most and least activity. As morning drew near, they both laid down and got some sleep. When they woke up, they watched and listened some more as they had something to eat and discussed what direction they thought would be their best bet for getting past the gangs unnoticed. Once they had formulated a plan, they waited for darkness to fall, and then they were on their way.

Raphael said, "We've had easy going for the last few days. I expect it's not going to be that way much longer. We need to take it slow and careful, now. We're going to head in that direction, where it sounds like there's less activity, but trouble could be anywhere. The route marked on the map doesn't mean much until we get past most of the bad guys. We will get back on course after we have done that, okay?"

Sonya said, "Sounds like a plan."

They were leaving the relative quiet of the residential area and heading into a part of the suburb made up of more businesses. That meant it would be an area of more interest to the gangs, since there was more to loot here. The farther they went, the closer the sounds became. Every once in a while, they would stop for a few minutes, just to listen. Then, they would adjust their course towards wherever sounded like less activity. They also paid close attention to whether or not there were signs of damage to the buildings, and looting. The more it looked like the gangs had already been there, the safer they felt, since that probably meant the gangs had already moved on. They stayed in the shadows as much as possible by traveling through back alleys and parking lots, behind businesses, rather than risking being seen out in front of the buildings, streetside. Progress was excruciatingly slow. It was hard to stay patient. They both wanted to put all of this behind them as soon as possible. But they both knew that this was not the time to get in a rush.

Sonya said, “I really thought we would have made it through here in one night, but now I’m not so sure.”

Raphael said, “Yeah, I know, right? It seems like they are moving almost at the same speed as we are. We’re gaining on them, but not as fast as I thought we would. I mean, I’m just fine with not having to run into any of them, but it’s bound to happen eventually. Just, maybe not tonight.”

Sonya said, “We’ve been going for hours, now, and we only have a couple more hours before morning. I think we need to find someplace to spend another day before we try to get past them.”

Raphael said, “I think you’re right. Let’s try to get just a little farther. And we’ll keep our eyes open for a good spot to spend the day. When we find some place, we’ll stop.”

They went on for about an hour and managed to find a deserted tattoo parlor on the second floor of a run-down building. With only one stairway leading up, it was about as good a place as any to spend the day. They snacked on some of the food which Frank had sent with them, and while he was eating, Raphael was checking out some of the stuff around the room. Sonya was rummaging through her pack when she suddenly heard, “Buzzzz, buzz, buzzzzzzz.”

She said, “What the heck?”

Raphael said, “Hey, check it out. It still works. Would you like a tattoo?”

Sonya said, “Yeah, uh, I don’t think so. I trust you, but not for that.”

He said, “Whaddayamean? I did tattoos for the guys, back in the day. I was pretty good at it, too.”

She said, "Seriously? Uh, yeah, I don't know. I don't think I really need a tattoo."

He said, "Ah, c'mon, let me just draw it with this marker so you can see what it would look like."

She said, "I guess there would be no harm in that." Then she pulled up the leg of her jeans and pointed to the side of her calf, and said, "Okay, right there."

He drew for a few minutes and said, "There, see, that looks good on you."

She looked at what he had drawn. It said, "Sonya & Raphael, Friends Forever." Her eyes welled up a little and she gave him a big hug, saying, "That's so sweet! And it's so true. We are friends, forever. If I was going to get a tattoo, that's exactly what it would be."

He asked, "So, whaddya say? Are you ready?"

She said, "I don't need a tattoo to remember our friendship. That will be with me, in my heart, forever, just like you will be."

He said, "Okay, but I was definitely looking forward to doing that tattoo!" Sonya said, half giggling, "Yeah, maybe just a little too much!"

They talked for a little longer, then settled in for some rest. Sonya laid down on the tattooing chair towards the back of the room. Raphael took the cushions from a couch and made them into a makeshift bed just around the corner from the top of the stairs. He always put himself in a position where he felt he could best protect Sonya, if he needed to. He truly cared for her, very much, and was always very protective of her. This didn't go unnoticed by Sonya. She thought of him as the big brother she never had. Even though she knew that she was just as likely to protect him as the other way around, she never said or did anything to make him feel any less the protector.

Just as she was about to drift off to sleep, realizing where she was lying, she said, "Just because I am in this chair, don't you get any crazy ideas while I'm asleep! No tattoo!"

Raphael let out an evil, "Heh, heh, heh," giving her a menacing look. Then he chuckled. She squinted her eyes, while shaking her finger at him, saying, "Don't even think about it!"

They were both thinking as they fell asleep about just how good of a friendship had grown between them. They were both equally grateful for the bond they had with one another.

They slept soundly through a totally uneventful day. As evening was approaching, they woke up, had some food, and walked around the room, stopping at each window to look and listen for any signs of what might be happening outside. It started out fairly quiet, but as night began to fall, there were more and more sounds coming from the surrounding area. By the time it was totally dark outside, they had determined which direction they needed to go. They gathered their things into their packs, and headed outside. The activity was obviously much closer to their location than it had been for the past several nights. They knew that this meant they would most likely be trying to get past the gangs tonight. This would, no doubt, be the most dangerous part of their entire journey.

Sonya said, "I think this is it. It's make or break time."

Raphael said, "I think you're right. If we can just get through this business district and into the residential area beyond that, I really believe that will put us past the worst of the gang activity. We need to be super careful, but we kinda have to keep moving at the same time. We sure don't want to get hung up somewhere in the middle of the danger zone. That would not be a good place to be stuck hiding through a day. We need to push through this, tonight!"

"Yep," Sonya said.

Raphael said, "Our goal, then, should be to make it to a safe hiding spot, somewhere as soon as we put these assholes behind us, okay? But until then, we keep moving."

Sonya said, "Sounds like a plan. It seems to be quieter in that direction. Let's go."

They were moving as quickly as caution would allow. They still stopped and listened to their surroundings frequently, but these stops were kept short. They didn't have a minute to spare if they were to achieve the goal they had set for themselves. The route they had chosen proved to be a good one. There was definitely activity, both to their left and to their right, but relative quiet ahead of them.

As they moved forward, they noticed that the sounds they heard on either side went from being ahead of them, to either side, to being beside them, to either side, to being behind them, to either side. As they made it even farther, the majority of the noise began to fade behind them.

Raphael said, "Whaddayaknow, I think we actually did it! I think we managed to put the worst behind us."

Sonya said, "Yeah, I think you're right. I can't believe we got through there so fast!"

Raphael said, "Now, as long as we have a few more hours of darkness, I think we should use that time to put as much distance between us and all of that back there as possible."

"Agreed," Sonya said, as she couldn't help but give

Raphael a giant hug.

As they were walking across the parking lot of this last business before getting to the residential area ahead, they suddenly heard footsteps behind them. Looking back, they could see two people running directly towards them. Sonya and Raphael started to run towards a short brick wall at the edge of the parking lot. Sonya said, "I don't see any guns, do you?"

Raphael said, "I don't think so."

Sonya could see that there was a downhill slope past the wall. She said, "Follow my lead."

Raphael said, "Got it."

Sonya jumped the wall and immediately dropped to the ground, quickly hiding behind the wall.

Raphael did the same. As their pursuers jumped the wall, Sonya and Raphael reached up and grabbed their feet causing both to faceplant into the ground. Then they each landed punches rendering both of the chasers unconscious.

Raphael said, "Shit, they're just kids."

Sonya said, "Yeah. No need to do more. By the time they wake up, we'll be long gone."

Raphael said, "They were probably just going to try to intimidate us into giving up some supplies, or something."

"Probably," Sonya said.

They continued ahead into the residential area, which had been their goal for about another hour. They had agreed that once they found a hiding spot for the next day, they would sleep in shifts, so that one of them would always be listening and watching to make sure the gangs weren't catching back up to them. There was no way they wanted that to happen, and they would move farther ahead long before that happened, if it became necessary. That was the plan, anyway.

They had made very good progress into the residential area and decided to look for their hiding spot, since there was now only about an hour left before daylight. Suddenly, there was the sound of a vehicle approaching, FAST! They had been so careful up until now, but for the first time, they had gotten careless. Maybe it was the rush of what they had just accomplished. Maybe they had just gotten a little too comfortable with their present surroundings, compared to where they had just been. But, for whatever reason, they were out on the street in the open, and didn't have many choices for places to get out of sight. Sonya managed to dive under a truck parked nearby. Raphael had tried to do the same, but the vehicle's headlights hit him before he could get there. From under the truck, Sonya couldn't see what was happening, but she stayed out of sight. Raphael was now hiding behind the truck as the vehicle screeched to a stop on the opposite side. He could see that there were four men in the vehicle and they looked to be gang members. He quietly retrieved the gun from his pack and prepared for a fight. All four doors on the car could be heard opening and slamming shut in unison. Sonya could only see their feet, but knew this was real trouble. She also knew that from where she was, she could do nothing. Suddenly, three shots rang out. From under the truck, Sonya saw the lifeless bodies of three of the men hit the ground. Then another shot rang out. But this one sounded different and was from the opposite direction. As she turned to look out from under the other side of the truck, she saw Raphael lying on the sidewalk, bleeding profusely from his neck. His gun was in his hand, reaching out to hand it to her. The look in his eyes was as if to tell her, “You have to!” She knew what she had to do. She may not have liked guns, but that didn’t mean she was oblivious as to how to use one. She took the gun, knowing that Raphael had only fired three rounds. This meant that there were at least six rounds left, maybe more. At this point, she was scared enough and angry enough to use a gun. These men had just shot her friend. No way was she about to let them get away with it! Knowing that only one of them was still standing, she aimed at all she could see, which was his feet, and rapidly fired four rounds, striking him twice. As he fell to the ground, looking right at her, she put two more rounds right between his eyes. She quickly crawled out from under the truck and rushed to where Raphael was. She cradled his head on her lap, trying to do whatever she could to stop the bleeding.

Raphael was barely able to say anything at all, but he managed to get out a few words, saying, “I’m not going to be able to help you any more. You have to go the rest of the way on your own. Now, hurry up and get out of here.”

Sonya said, “I’m not leaving you. You’re going to be okay.”

“I love you, sister,” he said with his last breath. His eyes went lifeless, and he was gone.

“I love you, too, brother,” she said as she closed his eyes with a gentle touch of her hand. She began to cry uncontrollably. She had never experienced the loss of someone she cared so much about.

She knew she needed to get the hell away from there before daylight, but she couldn’t leave Raphael just lying in the street. She spotted a church about a half block away, and with every ounce of her strength, she half dragged, half carried her friend's body to that church. She got him inside, and laid him down in front of the altar. She took some flowers out of a nearby vase and arranged them around Raphael. Then she sat down next to her friend and had one last conversation with him, just knowing that wherever he was, he was listening. She said, "I don't know if you were religious at all, but I got you here so you wouldn't have to do any more traveling to meet God.

You have earned your rest and I pray that you can be at peace now. Everything I do from now on is only possible because of you. I would have never made it this far without you, and I will thank you every day for the rest of my life for all that you did for me. Rest easy knowing that I am going to get out of here. I wish you could still be with me, but, in a way, you always will be. Thank you, brother." She had fought through her tears to say what she wanted to say, but she was now weeping so bitterly that she could say no more.

It was daylight outside by this time, so she decided to hide in this church until the next night.

She made her way up to the choir loft which would be the safest place to be, with only one way up. From here, she could look down and see her friend below. She had taken her pack and Raphael's pack with her and was beginning to consolidate the contents of both into hers. It felt strange to be rummaging through his pack, but she knew he would want her to take whatever she could use. Occasionally, she would stop, look down at Raphael, and run through the many memories they had created together. She went back and forth between laughing and crying, for hours. Sometimes, she would find herself talking to him, just as if he was still right there with her. As she was sitting there, the leg of her jeans had hiked up slightly, uncovering the smudged remains of the mock tattoo that Raphael had drawn. She said, "Ya know, brother, I really wish I had let you make this a real tattoo. Someday, I am going to get that tattoo, to honor you." Then the tears started flowing again, and she eventually cried herself to sleep.

# CHAPTER NINE

## SONYA, MEET A FEW GOOD PEOPLE

As had become the norm, Sonya woke up about an hour before the sun set on another day. She was finding something to eat from her pack when she looked down to where Raphael's body was, and saw someone standing over him, reaching down to touch him. She quietly snuck down from her hiding place in the choir loft to find out who this was messing with her friend. She walked up to within a few feet behind the person and said, "Who the fu…" As the man turned, she could see, from his collar, that he was a priest. She said, "Oh, I'm so sorry Father. I had no idea who you were."

"I'm Father Joseph," he replied.

"I'm Sonya," she said.

He said, "I was just saying a blessing over this poor man. Friend of yours?"

She replied, "Yes, his name is Raphael. He was my best friend. Thanks for the blessing, Father."

"You brought him here?" he asked.

Sonya replied, "Yeah, he was killed just down the street, yesterday, while protecting me. I couldn't bear to leave him out in the street. I saw your church and thought it would be a much better place for him to be."

Father Joseph said, "I could tell by the way he was lying here with the flowers around him that someone must have

truly cared about him."
Sonya said, "Yeah, I cared for him very much. I haven't known him for very long, but he was truly the best friend I have ever had. I wouldn't be here without him. He gave his life for me." Sonya began to cry and Father Joseph offered her a tissue and tried to comfort her. She then asked, "Can you make sure he has a proper burial?"

"Of course, my child," he said.

"Thank you, Father," she said.

Father Joseph asked, "May I have his full name and date of birth for the headstone?"

She said, "I don't even know all of that. Like I said, I haven't known him for long."

He asked, "Well, then, what should I have put on his headstone?"

She said, "Maybe just 'Raphael, A true friend. A good man. RIP.'"

"Okay, I'll see to it," he said.

"Thank you, again, Father. I really must be going, now," she said.

He asked, "It's getting dark out. Where are you going?"

She said, "It's a long story, Father. I've been traveling at night to get as far away from the city as possible. It's safer to use the cover of darkness to stay out of sight. The gangs are taking over more and more of the city, and are now also moving into the suburbs. Raphael helped me to get past them and I must keep going to stay ahead of them. They are not far behind me and they are coming this way. It's already getting bad here, but it's much, much worse back where I came from. I hope you will do whatever you can to stay safe. All I know is that I really have to get moving."

He said, "I would like to say a blessing for you, if you're okay with that."

She said, "Sure, Father. I'll take all the help I can get!"

With that, Father Joseph placed his hand on Sonya's head and prayed for her for a few minutes. Then he handed her a necklace with a medal on it. He said, "This is a Saint Christopher medal. He is the Patron Saint of travellers. He will protect you, wherever you go."

Sonya said, "Thank you, Father." Then she gave Father Joseph a hug, turned, and walked out of the church.

As Father Joseph watched her walk away, he made a sign of the Cross, and said, "Bless you, my child. May God be with you."

As Sonya left the church, she could hear the sounds of gang activity back where she had come from. Thankfully, it was quite a distance away. But she had learned a hard lesson from the death of her friend, and was not going to get careless or over-confident. She would be more careful than ever before as she began to move ever farther away from the violence behind her. She got back to using the shadows of the alleys and back yards to stay out of sight. She couldn't help but to think about just how alone she felt. Sure, she had started this journey alone, but she had become so accustomed to having Raphael with her. Now that he was gone, she felt more lonely than she had ever felt in her entire life. She often found herself talking to him as if he was still there. It seemed to help her cope with the fact that he wasn't.

She was quickly making her way through one neighborhood after another. At one point, she stopped to rest for a moment and to listen for any signs of activity. She pulled the map out of her pack and realized that she was now at the very outer edge of what Raphael had drawn for her. She put the map back in her pack, saying to herself, “Well, I guess that’s it for the map. I’ve made it. I’ve really made it!” In her mind, she could hear Raphael’s voice telling her that she still needed to be careful. She said, “I know, brother.”

Sonya got her stuff back together and continued on. She didn’t want to waste any more time. It had been so hard to get to the relative safety of where she now found herself. So, she wanted to keep gaining as much ground as possible between herself and the trouble behind her. As she was dashing across a street from one alley to the one on the other side, a shot rang out and a bullet splattered on the brick wall of the building right beside her. She had carefully checked the street in both directions before she crossed, and saw no one. She thought, “Where in the hell did that come from?” Her only choice now was to run like hell! Her only hope was to use her speed and agility to outrun and outmanoeuvre the shooter. She was going as fast as her feet would carry her, and making frequent direction changes to try to lose whoever this was behind her. More shots were fired and more bullets landed way too close for comfort, but fortunately, all missed. Suddenly, as she rounded a turn into an alley, several shots rang out from in front of her! She saw the muzzle flashes in the darkness ahead of her and they were coming from at least three different places. She thought to herself, “Well, this is it. This is how it ends. I ain’t getting out of this one.” She was certain that she was about to reunite with Raphael, right here, and right now. Three more shots came from in front of her, and she could hear the bullets whizzing over her head. She looked back over her shoulder to see where the person chasing her was, just in time to see him fall to the ground. As she turned back to look in front of her, three heads appeared, slowly rising above the rooflines of two houses, about a hundred yards ahead of her. Not sure what to make of what had just happened, Sonya put her hands in the air, and froze in place. A figure emerged from the darkness near the three heads she could see up on the rooftops. As this person approached Sonya, it became apparent that it was a woman, in full military gear.

She said, "I'm Captain Rose Phillips, United States Marines. Who are you and where are you heading?"

Sonya replied, "I'm Sonya. I am just passing through on my way out of the city and away from all that is going on back there. You just saved my life. Thank you."

Rose asked, "Where did you come from?"

Sonya explained that she had come all the way from the center of the city. Rose could hardly believe that Sonya had survived such a journey through so much trouble and danger.

Rose said, "You're lucky to be alive, considering the places you have travelled through."

Sonya said, "Oh, I know. I had some very good people help me along the way, especially one very good friend."

Rose asked, "Where is this friend, now?"

Sonya replied, "He didn't make it. He died, just yesterday, protecting me. It really hurts to know that he got so close to making it out. He said there were people, like you, out here, trying to stop the gangs from expanding any farther out."

Rose said, "Yeah, we're doing what we can. It's getting harder and harder to hold them back. They send out scouts to check out the areas ahead of them. That's most likely who was chasing you. There have been more of them out here lately. By the way, I'm sorry about your friend. Why don't you come over here and meet the rest of our group?"

By the time Rose had led Sonya to meet the others, they had come down off the roofs. Rose began to introduce everyone. She said, "This is Greg Haines, formerly a police officer from the city. Over here, we have Josh Carlson, US Army, retired. He's a resident of this area, trying to protect the town he loves. And last, but not least, we have Scott Paulson, Navy Seals, active duty - well, at least until all of this happened. Everyone, this is Sonya."

Sonya went around the group shaking their hands and thanking them, but hesitated a bit when Scott extended his hand. He asked, "What is it? Something wrong?"

She said, "No, it's nothing. It's just that I knew a Navy Seal once. It didn't go so well."

Rose said, "Trust me. He's one of the good guys. They all are."

Sonya said, "Yeah, I know. I'm sorry. I didn't mean any disrespect. Thank you all for saving my life."

Greg asked, "So where are you planning to go from here? There's not much going on past here."

Sonya said, "Somewhere with not much going on sounds absolutely perfect to me. I'm just looking for a peaceful existence where I don't have to be looking over my shoulder, constantly worrying about what's gonna happen next. And somewhere out there, I have family. At least, I hope they're out there somewhere. I had to leave them behind when I left the city. My friend told me that groups like you had helped as many people as they could to escape the city and the gangs. He told me to never give up hope that they had made it to safety.

And I never have. It's the only thing keeping me going. He made a map for me, showing what directions I could go to look for them if I made it this far. So, that's exactly what I am going to do. I will keep looking for as long as it takes."

Josh said, "Let me see that map. Maybe we can point you in the right direction."

Rose said, "Yeah, if you can show us on that map where you came from, we might be able to show you where the most likely spots are that your family could have been taken. Before we teamed up, we came from different places. Maybe one of us can spot something on your map that will help us to help you."

Rose, Greg, Josh, and Sonya all gathered around the map. Scott, sensing that Sonya seemed pretty uncomfortable with him, stayed back a bit. Once they all understood what part of the city Sonya had come from, Rose said, "Hey, Scott, come over here and have a look. I think Sonya came from not far from where you said you were, before you teamed up with us."

Scott walked over, looked at where they were all pointing on the map, and said, "Yeah, I was there a while back. Anyone who was rescued from that area most likely would have been taken here." He was pointing to an imaginary point about six inches off the edge of Sonya's map.

Rose said, "You couldn't be much more on the opposite side of the city from there than you are right now."

Sonya said, "I only ended up here because it was the safest route out of the city that my friend knew of. I had no way to know that it was going to take me farther from the place my family might possibly end up."

Josh said, "Well, you obviously took the right way out.

You survived, after all, right?"

Greg said, "Yeah, and we're glad you made it out."

Rose said, "Oh yeah, absolutely! All I'm saying is that you have a long way to go."

Scott added, "Especially when you consider that you need to take the long way around," as he drew a long, sweeping arc with his finger, well off the edge of the map.

Sonya said, "Well, there's no doubt that I will take the long way around. Besides, I may find other places to check for them along the way."

Rose said, "You should rest here with us for the day. The four of us have been to lots of places that your map doesn't show. We can put our heads together to make an updated map for you. We can show the way to several places where you can go to look for your family. We can also show where there are other teams, like us, who may be able to help you further. Otherwise, you will be flying blind."

Sonya said, "That would be awesome! Thanks to all of you for helping me out."

As Greg, Josh, and Scott grabbed a large sheet of paper and began drawing up a map, complete with helpful notes and approximate locations of other teams, as well as marking "no-go" areas, Rose and Sonya sat and talked for hours. Rose saw Sonya about to eat some MREs from her pack, and stopped her, saying, "I've got something much better than that crap, for you to eat. C'mon, let's get some real food into you." She lit a camp stove and prepared a good hot meal for Sonya. Not since Sonya and Raphael had been at Frank's house had she eaten so well.

Sonya said, "Thanks. That really hit the spot."

Rose said, "It looks like the guys have about finished their contributions to your new map. I'm going to go over and add my touches to it, okay?"

Sonya said, "Sure. Thanks."

Scott slowly approached Sonya and said, "Regardless of whatever bad experience you had with a Seal in the past, just know that we're generally good guys."

Sonya said, "I know. I'm sorry. I shouldn't have acted that way towards you."

Scott said, "Just my gut feeling, but I want you to pay particular attention to the location I marked on the map. If your family is anywhere, my money is on that location. You will be passing many of these so-called 'safe zones' on your way. And you will want to check them all, in case I am wrong. But your focus, in my opinion, should be on that spot. As you get closer to that spot, talk to the teams who are nearby. They may be able to help you."

"Okay, I'll do that. Thanks," Sonya said.

Rose returned carrying the map which they had put together for Sonya. She said, "I hope this helps. You've got a long road ahead of you. You'll need your rest. You can hang out with us as long as you want before you go."

Sonya said, "Thanks, but I should get going tonight as soon as it's dark."

"As soon as it's dark?" Rose asked.

Sonya said, "Yeah, I travel at night to avoid being seen. It's worked well, so far, for the most part."

Rose said, "You really won't need to hide in the dark beyond this point. You're entering a whole different world from here on out. Sure, you'll need to still be careful, but where you're going now, you'd be better off traveling during daylight. You wouldn't believe how hard it is to navigate out there in the dark. You'll need to be able to see where you're going."

Well, that will take some getting used to, for me," Sonya said.

Rose said, "Get some rest. We got you covered. Relax for the rest of today, then try to get some sleep tonight. Then tomorrow morning, after I make you a good breakfast, you can be on your way."

Sonya spent the rest of the day talking with her new friends. They shared their meals with her and treated her like one of the family. They offered her lots of advice on her upcoming adventure. She absorbed every word like a sponge. Between the four of them, they had knowledge about most of the areas she was about to travel through. She took it all in, committing it all to memory, and making notes on her new map. As evening approached, out of habit, she began gathering her belongings into her pack.

Rose gave her a look as if to ask where she was going.

Sonya said, "Ya know, I've done this so many times that I actually forgot that I'm not leaving until morning."

Rose said, "Yeah, I kinda figured that."

Sonya said, "I haven't actually slept at night for so long, I'm not sure if I can."

Rose pulled a flask out of her pocket and said, "This might help."

Sonya took a sip and started coughing. "Wow!" she said. Rose said, "Good, huh?"

Sonya giggled, took another sip, and said, "Yeah, really smooth." She passed the flask back to Rose, still coughing.

Rose laughed, took a big swig from the flask and passed it back to Sonya, saying, "It might not be the best, but it will help you sleep."

They passed the flask back and forth several times, both giggling a little more each time. They talked some more until, eventually, the flask was empty. Rose said she had to go use the little girls' room, and when she returned, Sonya was sound asleep. Rose covered Sonya with a blanket, whispering, "I told you it would help you sleep." Rose went to check on Greg, Josh, and Scott.

They had taken up their positions on the rooftops, keeping watch. Satisfied that the guys had the situation under control, Rose went to get some sleep, too.

As Rose was trying to get to sleep, she would look over at Sonya and wonder how in the world this young girl could have possibly survived the journey she had been on. "She must be tougher than she looks," Rose thought to herself, "When I was that age, I wouldn't have made it through my first day out there." She had no idea just what kind of fabric Sonya was cut from.

# CHAPTER TEN

## SONYA, MEET NEW FRIENDS

Rose, being an early riser, was up at five a.m. After checking on the guys, she went about preparing breakfast for the group. The camp stove just happened to be directly upwind from Sonya. The irresistible aromas reaching Sonya, especially the coffee, had her awake in no time.

Sonya walked over to Rose and said, "That coffee smells fantastic. I love my coffee in the morning and I have missed it so much. I've only had it once during my entire journey when a very kind man let Raphael and myself stay with him for a couple days."

Rose asked, "Raphael? Is that the friend you mentioned, who didn't make it?"

"Yeah," Sonya replied, "he was a true friend. We didn't know each other for very long, but he was like a big brother to me. He gave his life for me. I miss him a lot."

Rose said, "Yeah, I'm sure you do. I'm so sorry you lost your friend. I've lost lots of friends, too. It sucks. All you can do is to carry on and keep the good memories of them in your heart. Then you eventually make new friends, just like you have with us. We won't be together long enough to really grow on each other, but I would like to count you as one of my friends and I hope you think of us as friends, too."

Sonya said, "I definitely think of you as friends. You saved my life. I wish I could repay you, somehow."

Rose said, "No need. That's what we're here for. Knowing we helped you when you needed help is all the repayment we need. It gives us a sense of purpose. What else would we do?"

Sonya said, "Well anyway, thanks."

Rose said, "Breakfast is ready so you go ahead and help yourself while I go let the guys know."

Sonya grabbed a cup of coffee and a heaping plate of what Rose had made. Rose returned with Greg, Josh, and Scott in tow. By the time they got their plates, Sonya had devoured her breakfast and was sipping on her second cup of coffee. She sat and talked with them while they ate their breakfast. All of them shared more tips and suggestions with Sonya regarding her upcoming adventure.

Scott said, "You have a lot of miles ahead of you if you follow the safest route which we laid out for you. And I suggest you follow that route as closely as possible. Don't be tempted to take any shortcuts."

Greg said, "Always keep in mind which direction you are from the city. If you veer off course at all, make sure it takes you farther away, not closer."

Josh added, "Make sure to stop at every 'safe zone' you pass. Even if your family isn't there, you can at least ask questions. They just might have some helpful information about what lies ahead of you."

Rose said, "And you just might find a good hot cup of coffee there, too. Probably not as good as mine, though!"

Sonya smiled and said, "Yep, your coffee would be hard to beat!"

The three guys mumbled and cleared their throats, teasing Rose about her coffee, like it really wasn't that good. Rose informed them that if they didn't like her coffee, they were welcome to make it themselves. Then they all acted like it was the best they had ever had and had a laugh.

Rose said, "Yeah, I thought so."

Sonya said, "Well, I guess I better get going. Thank you all again, for everything." Then she shouldered her pack and said her goodbyes, shaking hands with each of them. Scott and Josh went back to their positions on the rooftops while Greg settled in for some sleep. Rose was up for her turn to help with lookout duty, but first, she walked with Sonya for about the first block.

Then Rose stopped and said, "Well you're on your own from here. Best of luck and stay safe. Go find your family."

Sonya gave Rose a hug and said, "That's the plan. Thanks."

Then she turned and walked away. It was going to feel strange, traveling during daylight after only moving at night for so long. But she had been assured by her newest friends that it was the best time to travel from here on out. Looking at the new map she had been given, she could see that there were many more places where groups of good people were doing the same thing as Rose's group were doing. She had to trust that they were keeping the chaos and violence from spreading any farther out. The more ground she covered, the more she believed that to be the case. She was moving along quite quickly, compared to the pace she had gotten accustomed to. Out of habit, she would occasionally stop and listen. Not a sound, except for the sounds of nature, was to be heard.

It was late afternoon when Sonya decided to look for a

place to spend the night. There was a small house ahead and she walked towards it, keeping her ears and eyes open for any sign of life.

As she got closer, she could see that it was pretty run down. The grass hadn't been mowed, it was all overgrown with bushes and shrubs, half of the paint was peeling off, and the mailbox was hanging upside down by one rusty nail. It sure looked abandoned, but she still approached very slowly and cautiously. Ever so slowly, she opened the door and carefully went inside. "Oh, yeah, it's abandoned, alright," she said to herself. She had a look around, just to confirm that she was alone, and once satisfied that she was, she went upstairs. Old habits die hard. She made sure to find a room with more than one way out. What was left of the wallpaper on the walls made it obvious that this had been a little girl's bedroom. The window led out onto a roof, which wasn't high off the ground, in case she had to make a hasty exit. "This will do," she thought.

She opened her pack to find something to eat and to her surprise, there was a rolled-up blanket, a few candles, and some matches, right on top. There was a note saying, "Didn't want you to be cold in the dark. Rose." It brought a tear to her eye to think how nice some people can still be. She had something to eat, propped her pack against the wall to lay against, and covered up with the blanket. Having opened the window, she marvelled at just how quiet it was here. The only sounds were the frogs and crickets singing outside. Looking out the window, she immediately understood why Rose and the others had told her to travel during the day. She had never experienced such total darkness. It was so new to her that she actually had to get back up and crawl out onto the roof outside the window to have a look. Spending her entire life in the city, she had never seen the night sky like this. She said to herself, "Who knew there were so many stars? No wonder some people want to live out here! It's absolutely beautiful!" She actually considered sleeping right out there on that roof, but as the chilly night air began to feel colder, she opted for going back in and under that blanket. Before long, she was fast asleep. She had covered a lot of miles that day, and was more tired than she even knew.

Sonya hadn't slept this soundly for a long, long time. In fact, she couldn't remember the last time she had experienced a dream. She had rarely been in a deep enough sleep for a dream to have a chance of happening for weeks. But now, she was actually dreaming. She was dreaming that someone with a really bad cold, who couldn't stop sniffling, was trying to pull her pack from behind her. Then someone else with an equally bad cold and case of the sniffles was trying to pull her pack out from the opposite direction. She was sleep mumbling, "I don't have any cold medicine in my pack. Leave my pack alone." Her own mumblings brought her to a half-awake state and when she partially opened her eyes, she saw two sets of eyes staring back at her from either side! Startled, she jumped and woke up the rest of the way, ready for a fight. As her vision cleared up a bit, she could see that on each side of her were two of the prettiest Malinoises she had ever seen. They were sitting about two feet to either side of her, heads both cocked to one side, looking alternately at her and her pack. One look at those puppy dog eyes told Sonya just what they wanted. They had been smelling the food in her pack, and trying to get at it as she slept. Sonya said, "If you would just ask politely, instead of trying to steal my food, maybe I would give you something." They both laid down staring up at Sonya. There were those eyes, again! She said, "There, now that's more like it. Where did you two come from, anyway?" Until now, she wasn't sure exactly why she had kept that bag of dog treats in her pack. But these two sure appreciated the fact that she did! She checked them for tags, but found none. One was male and the other, female. Their markings led Sonya to believe that they could well be brother and sister. They were like mirror images of one another. They seemed to be healthy, but more than a little bit hungry. They had shown no sign of aggression, so Sonya didn't feel any fear of them. Sonya had something to eat herself, and shared a few bites with them. It was getting light outside, so Sonya said, "I've gotta go. You two, go home." As she started walking, it was soon obvious that they intended to go with her. She said, "Look, it's all I can do to find enough to eat myself. I can't afford two more mouths to feed. Go home." Nothing she said had any effect whatsoever. They just kept following her. She even tried to lunge at them and raise her voice, "GO HOME!" They took it as play time and lunged back, stopping short of her and looking up with "those eyes".

Remembering what Raphael had told her about how valuable a good dog can be, and how he had ended up with Zola at his side, she finally accepted the fact that these two had their minds made up. He had said, "I gave her some food and a little attention, and that was it. She stayed right by my side from that day on." She realized that she had just done the same exact thing with these two.

Sonya said, "Okay, you two can come along. But you're gonna have to earn your keep. I may not always have a lot of food to share with you, so you might have to find food for yourselves, sometimes." Realizing that what they were hearing was probably, "blah blah bla ba ba blah", she said, "Okay, let's go." If nothing else, it felt good to have someone to talk to.

Sonya knew, from consulting the map which Rose, Josh, Greg, and Scott had made for her, that the dirt road she was traveling was right on the line between where to be and where not to be. A little farther ahead, she would be coming to a main road which led into one of the suburbs. To the right, that road would lead into that suburb. She would be going left. After following that road for about a half-mile, she would resume her original direction of travel on another back road. The plan was to stay away from main roads as much as possible. If any bad guys were to get past the small groups trying to keep them contained, they would most likely be on the main roads. So, the back roads were a much safer place to be.

She walked along with her two new traveling companions, one on her left and one on her right. They were walking beside her as if they had been with her forever. At one point she had passed an apple tree, loaded with beautiful red apples. She had picked a bunch and stuffed as many as she could into her pack. She knew that she had better load up on any kind of food she could, whenever she could, since there would be fewer opportunities to do so out here. She stopped and took an apple out to snack on as she walked along. Her new companions gave her a look with those puppy dog eyes again, and she wondered, "Can dogs eat apples?" She cut one in half, removed the core, and put them down to see if these dogs seemed interested. They gobbled them up like candy. "Okay, so dogs like apples, I guess," she said to herself.

When she had made it to about a half mile short of that

main road, she could hear several gunshots, far in the distance, to her right. She stopped and listened for a few minutes to see if she would hear any more. After hearing nothing more, she continued on. She figured one of those groups, similar to the group which had saved her life, must have had an encounter with some gang bangers trying to get past them. Not knowing for sure which side had won, she proceeded with just a little more caution. When she could see the main road, she decided to stay off to the side of it while keeping it in sight, just in case she needed to quickly take cover. Ducking under trees and through bushes and brush, she made her way until the back road, which she was going to follow, was in sight on the opposite side of the main road. After carefully looking down the main road to make sure no one was coming, she decided to dash across as quickly as possible. Just as she reached the other side, a man, with a gun pointed at her, came running out of the bushes near the intersection of the back road and the main road. Her two companions immediately dashed into the bushes, one to the left and one to the right. As Sonya put her hands up, she thought to herself, "Oh great, they've abandoned me!" As the man approached Sonya, still pointing his gun at her, he asked what was in her pack and demanded that she give it to him. All of a sudden, the two Malinoises, one from each side, launched an airborne attack on the man. One had the man's hand and gun clamped in his jaws, while the other had the man's throat clamped in her jaws. The guy had no idea what had just hit him. By the time Sonya ran over, he was disarmed and rapidly bleeding out. Sonya looked at the two dogs in utter amazement. They just looked back up at her as if to say, "What?" Sonya knelt down and gave them both a big hug to thank them for saving her life. She divided up one of those apples for them saying, "You both deserve a treat. I said you had to earn your keep. I would say that you just did."

Sonya and her two heroes continued down the back road for several hours. Evening was approaching and Sonya found a place to spend the night. She said to the two dogs, "You deserve to eat well, tonight, after what you did for me. So, tonight, we are having something special," She had two cans of beef stew in her pack and opened them both. She gave one to each of her new friends while she had some of the MREs for herself. "You two need names," she said. She thought long and hard, but couldn't think of any good names. Suddenly, it came to her. She wanted to honor her fallen friend and his fallen friend. She looked at the male Malinois and said, "I'm going to name you Raphael. But we'll just call you Rafe, for short." Then she looked at the female and said, "Your name will be Zola. Yes! Those are perfect names for you two," she said as she gave them both treats and said their new names over and over.

Sonya was tired and decided that it was time to get some sleep. She laid down and Rafe and Zola were practically squashing her as they laid down on either side of her. She pulled the blanket up over the entire trio and said, "Yep, Rafe and Zola, you certainly have earned your keep. And you've earned those two names, too. Those aren't just any old names, ya know. They are very special names. Raphael was my guardian angel. Zola was his guardian angel. Now, you are both my guardian angels." She gave both Rafe and Zola big hugs and belly rubs as they returned the affection with ample licks, kisses, and nuzzling, and soon, all three were sound asleep.

# CHAPTER ELEVEN

## SONYA, RAFE, AND ZOLA, MEET THE OUTSIDE WORLD

Shortly before morning, Sonya was having a dream in which she was washing her face with a nice, warm washcloth. She woke up to find that Rafe and Zola were vigorously licking her face from both sides. She said, "Okay, okay, you two, I'm up. Puh! Puh! Jeez! Let's see if you two know your names today." She got the last of the dog treats out of her pack and said, "Rafe, sit." Rafe immediately sat, perfectly.

Sonya gave him a treat and walked a few steps away. She said, "Rafe, come." Rafe walked over and sat down right in front of Sonya. Sonya said, "Good boy!" Sonya gave Rafe another treat and then said, "Zola, come." Zola went right to Sonya and looked up at her as if to say, "What, now?" Sonya gave her a treat and said, "Zola, sit." Zola sat perfectly and received a treat. Sonya said, "Awesome! You two are amazing!"

Sonya took out her map and was snacking on some food from her pack. Of course, she couldn't eat in peace without sharing a little with Rafe and Zola. According to the map, she should be reaching one of the "safe zones" later in the day. It was one of several which she would be visiting before getting anywhere near where her family were likely to be, if they had made it out at all. But it would take her even farther out from the city and any suburbs than she had been so far. That, in itself, was a good thing.

Farther out, in theory, meant safer. Also, she could possibly get some information, tips, and maybe some supplies. Supplies would be a real plus, since she now had extra mouths to feed.

Sonya said, “Rafe, Zola, you ready to go?” It took all of about two seconds for Rafe and Zola to be standing at Sonya’s side, waiting for their new friend’s next move. They were more than ready for whatever adventure Sonya had for them. And Sonya was so glad to have them by her side. It was good to not feel so alone any more.

Sonya, Rafe, and Zola were truly “out in the country”, now. They were walking past fields of vegetables, fruit orchards, and groves of nut trees. This came in quite handy, since Sonya could find things to eat without having to deplete the limited supplies which she had in her pack. She could also add some of these things to her pack to use later. After walking many miles, Sonya knew that they were getting close to one of the safe zones. They would be stopping there to see if they could rest there, and possibly get some information, and maybe some supplies. There was no chance of her family being here. It was still much too far from the side of the city she came from. There was, also, very little chance of any information being available here about her family. But information on what to expect between here and the next stop along the way would likely be available here.

As they got near, they were met by two soldiers who were patrolling the road leading to the camp.

One of them said, “I’m Corporal Sam Johnson, United States Army, and this is Private Joe Koslowski, United States

Army. Who are you and where are you heading?"
Sonya said, "My name is Sonya. These are my friends, Rafe and Zola. We are just traveling from one safe zone to another, looking for my family. They are most likely not in your camp, but the people that helped me out at the last place we were at suggested stopping at each safe zone along the way to rest, get information, and possibly some supplies. Your camp was the next stop according to the map they drew up for me. So, here we are."

Joe said, "Beautiful dogs you have there. They remind me of a dog that worked with my unit in Afghanistan."

Sonya said, "Thanks. I haven't had them with me for long, but they have already saved my life once. Now we're a team."

Sam said, "C'mon with us. You are welcome to get some rest. We can provide some supplies for you to take with you. We may not have much in the way of information for you, but we will help out however we can."

Sonya said, "Thanks. I appreciate it."

When they got to the camp, they soon discovered that there were two other dogs there. They greeted Rafe and Zola, and before long, the four dogs were engaging in play fights and chasing each other all over. But any time the other dogs headed away from where Sonya was, Rafe and Zola would stop, refusing to follow any farther. They would never let Sonya out of their sight. This was both amazing to Sonya and a relief to know at the same time.

Joe and Sam showed Sonya around the camp. There were several hundred people here who had been rescued from the violence and mayhem in the city. Sonya, although she knew her family was not at all likely to be here, looked carefully at every face she encountered, looking for any face which might be even remotely familiar. Not one face was familiar to her. This was no surprise and didn't in any way discourage her from continuing her quest.

Everyone was kind and welcoming. Several people offered Sonya various supplies, and before long her pack was filled to capacity. One kind lady even gave her several cans of dog food for Rafe and Zola. They made Sonya feel right at home, sharing a meal with her and providing a place for Sonya, Rafe, and Zola to sleep for the night. In the morning, there was breakfast and the invitation to stay as long as she wanted. Sonya thanked them all, then explained that she must keep moving to hopefully, someday, find her family.

Sonya, Rafe, and Zola began the trek to the next safe zone on her map, and the whole process was repeated again. Kind people gladly provided more supplies, a little more information, and helpful tips to help guide her along the way. This continued, day after day, safe zone after safe zone, for days. It was always amazing to Sonya just how many good people she met along the way. Maybe there was still hope for the human race, after all.

Looking at her map, Sonya could see that she was finally getting close to the safe zones where Rose, Greg, Josh, and Scott had told her she had the best chance of finding her family, if they had been moved out of the city. There were three more between her and the one which Scott had indicated as the most likely one of all. Sonya had decided that from this point on, she would spend at least a full day at each place. She wanted to make sure to lay eyes on every single face, of every single person in these last few safe zones. Of course, the hope was to find her family, but even finding a familiar face that she recognized from her old neighborhood could be extremely important. Someone that she knew might be able to shed light on the whereabouts of her mom, little brother, and little sister. They might be able to tell her if they had made it out at all. Sonya would leave no stone unturned from here on.

She approached the next safe zone, was greeted and checked out at the perimeter, as at every other place she had been to. Then she was welcomed into the camp where Rafe and Zola always managed to make friends almost immediately. If it wasn't with dogs, Rafe and Zola were always a huge hit with children, too. There was always someone to have some play time with and they absolutely loved every minute of it. They were gluttons for any kind of attention. But they continued to always keep Sonya in sight. Their friendly demeanour and playful spirit always resulted in their bellies being full.

Sonya, Rafe, and Zola spent the night and the next day and night here, making sure to meet every single person. Having not seen a single familiar face, it was time to continue on to the next safe zone when morning arrived. Sonya always made sure to thank everyone who had helped her before they left. Having done so, she said, "C'mon, Rafe, c'mon, Zola, time to go." Then off they went, towards the next place on the map.

Late the next afternoon, they arrived at the next safe zone. Sonya felt a little more excited at each place than the one before. She just felt, in her heart, that she was going to find her family at one of these places, any day now. She refused to let any negative thoughts enter her mind. THEY WERE GOING TO BE OKAY. And, SHE WAS GOING TO FIND THEM. That was that! PERIOD! As was the norm, she got the tour and was offered something to eat and a place to sleep for the night. About halfway through the next day, out of the corner of her eye, she thought she recognized someone. She spun around to investigate whether this was actually a familiar face, or just her wishful thinking causing her mind to play tricks on her. She followed this woman for a few minutes and the woman, sensing that she was being followed, turned around and asked, "Can I help you?"

Sonya asked, "Don't I know you?"

The woman said, "I don't think so. Wait a minute, you do look a little familiar. But I'm not sure from where."

Sonya asked, "Didn't you and your husband used to run a little store down the street from where we lived? Cuzzie's Corner Market? You're Mrs. Cuzzie, aren't you?"

She said, "Yes, that's right. I'm trying to place you. Your father was a Navy Seal, right? Your mom barely ever left the house. I never even knew her name. You had a little brother and a little sister. You used to come into our store to pick up things for your mom. Why, you're little Sonya, aren't you? No wonder I didn't recognize you. You're all grown up now."

Sonya said, "Yep. That's me. I'm glad to see you made it out okay. Is your husband here with you?"

"No," she said wiping a tear from her eye, "he was shot in the store one day before we were evacuated,"

"Oh, I'm so sorry," Sonya said.

Mrs. Cuzzie said, "Thank you. I really miss him. How about your family, are they okay?"

Sonya said, "I don't know for sure, but I feel like they are. I just need to find them. I had to leave without them, so I don't know what became of them after that. I've been traveling from safe zone to safe zone searching for them. I've been hoping to see someone that I recognize that I might be able to get information about my family from. You're the first familiar face I've seen. Have you seen my family or heard anything about them?"

Mrs. Cuzzie replied, "No, I'm sorry, but I don't have any information regarding your family.

What I can tell you, though, is this: People were getting evacuated from our neighborhood pretty regularly. We were taken to a camp which is two camps away from here. That's where I was, originally. As it got more and more crowded, some of us were moved on to the next camp. Eventually, that one became overcrowded, as well. That's when I ended up here. I believe people were being moved to a camp in the opposite direction, as well, when crowding became a problem. So, with so many people being evacuated, it's quite possible that your family could be in any one of the next three camps, especially if they were evacuated after I was. I wish I could help you, somehow."

Sonya said, "Oh, you have. Believe me. You have given me even more hope that my family might be okay. And you have given me another place to look for them. If I haven't found them in the next two safe zones, I will find out where this third one is and look there. So, thank you, so much."

Mrs. Cuzzie said, "I hope you find them. I'll be praying for you."

With that, Sonya gave Mrs. Cuzzie a hug and went to gather up Rafe and Zola from where they were playing with a group of children, having a grand time. They went back to the place they had been given to rest during their visit, and had something to eat. Then the three of them all curled up together for some much-needed sleep.

The next morning, after a great breakfast and an even greater cup of coffee, prepared by their gracious hosts, Sonya and her two best friends started their walk through the countryside towards their next destination. The anticipation of what was to come farther down the road was filling Sonya's entire body and soul with so much excitement that she almost didn't notice just how peaceful and beautiful it was out here. But she did notice. The more she was out in the open, the more she grew to love it. In fact, she had to ask herself why anyone would ever want to live in the city, even when times were good! She knew she would never live in a city again, even if things ever got back to normal. Out here is where she would call home from now on.

According to her map, the next safe zone wasn't as long of a hike to get to. It wouldn't require a full day of traveling to get to. And with a little extra time, Sonya thought they might have a little relaxing time at a lake which was on the map, not far ahead. When they got to the lake, it was so beautiful, with crystal clear water and a nice sandy beach. Sonya said, "Rafe, Zola, how about a swim?" They were in the water before Sonya could even get one article of clothing off. She stripped down to her underwear and joined Rafe and Zola for some much-needed downtime. It went without saying that Rafe and Zola were having fun, but Sonya realized just how much fun she was having.

She thought to herself, "Fun? I can't remember the last time I had fun. For a long, long time, all I have thought about is how to survive and how to just make it to the next day. This is how life should be."

They all splashed and played for about two hours. After

that, they had a little picnic on the beach, while just soaking up the beauty of their surroundings. Then it was time to move on. Sonya wanted to get to their destination before it got too late.
About two hours before sunset, they arrived at the next safe zone. Sonya said to Rafe and Zola, "Maybe today you'll get to meet your grandma! Yeah, you heard me right, your grandma. Since it looks like I've adopted you, I'm officially your mom. That makes my mom your grandma!" The tilt of their heads told Sonya that they probably heard, "Blah bla bla bla blah." Then she said, "Don't worry, you'll understand when it happens."
After being greeted by a couple people who were guarding the entrance to the camp, and the usual introductions had taken place, they were graciously invited in and given a place to rest. Since it was so late in the day by the time they had arrived, and that swim had them all pretty tired, they basically just ate and went to sleep. They would have a look around the next morning.

When morning arrived, Sonya was startled by the fact that Rafe and Zola were not squishing her from either side the way they normally did. In an almost panicked tone, Sonya called out, "Rafe, Zola, where are you?"

"They're fine, right over there," said a voice from right behind her.

Sonya turned to see who this was. She saw a smiling face and a cup of coffee being offered to her.

She said, "Thank you," as she looked where this person was pointing. Rafe and Zola were happily playing fetch with a couple of young children just a little way away.

"Those are a couple of great dogs you have there. My name is George, by the way," the man said.

She replied, "I'm Sonya. Nice to meet you."

George said, "I've been sitting here watching them play with those kids. If the kids throw the stick anywhere out of sight of you, they won't go after it. But as long as it's somewhere where they can see you, they will retrieve it, every time, without fail. They must have been with you for a long time to be so protective of you."

Sonya said, "No, actually, they haven't been with me all that long. But, yeah, they stick to me like glue. And they have saved my life once already."

George said, "Amazing! They sure are good with the kids, too. So, it looks like you are doing a bit of traveling. Where are you heading?"

Sonya said, "I've been going from one safe zone to another looking for my family. I had to leave them behind when I left the city and I am hoping that they made it to one of these places safely. After I have a look around here, if I haven't found them, I will move on to the next. Someone who helped me, a ways back, said the next one is the most likely place that they might be. But I need to look here first."

George said, "I can show you around, if you like."

"That would be great. Thanks," she said.

George asked, "How many safe zones have you checked?"

"I lost count, but several," she said.

He said, "There are more of these safe zones being established all the time. As more and more people are brought out of the city, they eventually get kinda crowded. So, people get moved to new places to make room. You said the next one is the most likely place to find your family. I'm guessing that's because the next one is the closest to where your family would have been brought out. Just keep in mind that they could have been moved in either direction after that. There are many more beyond the next. So, even if they're not here or at the next, don't lose hope, okay?"

Sonya said, "I'll never lose hope. I've come this far, so if I have to go even farther, that's what I will do."

"That's the spirit," George said.

They were walking as they talked, and Sonya was keeping an eye out for any familiar face. George was trying to make sure she got to lay eyes on every person in the camp. They had made it through about half of the camp without seeing a single familiar face. Suddenly, Sonya got a whiff of something that smelled delicious. She asked, "What is that I'm smelling?" George said, "Oh, that's Mrs. Yang's cooking that you're smelling. None of us can resist her food and she is all too happy to share with anyone who stops by. Are you hungry?"

Sonya said, "Are you kidding? I'm starved!"

George said, "C'mon, I'll introduce you."

Sonya said, "Okay."

"Good morning, Mrs. Yang. Something smells fantastic, as always. Meet our guest, Sonya," George said.

Mrs. Yang said, "Hello, Sonya. Won't you sit and have something to eat?"

Sonya said, "Nice to meet you, Mrs. Yang. I thought you'd never ask!"

Mrs. Yang, setting down a heaping plate in front of Sonya, said, "Here you are. Enjoy."

As Sonya was eating, she couldn't help but notice that Mrs. Yang kept staring at her and looked as if she was trying to remember something. Finally, Sonya just had to ask, "Have we met before? I mean, you keep looking at me as if you're trying to place me from somewhere."

Mrs. Yang said, "I'm so sorry. I don't mean to stare. You just look vaguely familiar. But I can't figure out from where or when."

Sonya asked, "What part of the city did you come from?"

Mrs. Yang explained where she had lived and went on to say, "I used to work in the kitchen at the Smiling Dragon restaurant."

Sonya said, "I remember that place from when I was a little girl. I used to beg to go there because I loved the big dragon statue in the driveway. I was only about five or six years old, then."

Mrs. Yang said, "Oh, you're the little girl that used to come with your mom and dad. She was a very pretty lady who looked like she might have been from South America or someplace like that. Your dad was a very handsome sailor, right?"

"Yeah, my dad was a sailor and my mom was from Puerto Rico," Sonya said.

Mrs. Yang said, "You always wanted the same thing. You loved my coconut shrimp. I don't know how many times I made that for you. But then there came a time when I never saw you and your family, any more."

Sonya said, "Once my little brother and sister came along, we didn't go out to eat as much. I must say, you haven't lost your touch. This food is fantastic. Who would have ever thought that I would be enjoying your cooking again, after all these years!" Then she asked, "Would you recognize my mom, if you saw her today? Is there any chance you may have seen her since you left the city?"

Mrs. Yang said, "It's been a long time since you and your

family used to eat at our restaurant, but now that you mention it, I did see a woman who looked familiar, just the way you did. At the time, I didn't give it much thought, but now, I think that could have been your mom. Did she come out of the city about a month ago, around the same time as I did?"

Sonya said, "That's just it, I don't know. I had to leave them behind when I left. I've been searching for them ever since. Did this woman have a little boy and girl with her?"

"Yes, she did. But there was no one else. Just a woman with two young children. No father," Mrs. Yang replied.

Sonya said, "Well, my father left us a while back."

Mrs. Yang said, "Oh, I'm so sorry to hear that. You were such a lovely family."

Sonya asked, "So, do you have any idea where they might be now?"

Mrs. Yang said, "This place was pretty crowded already when I got here. Pretty much everyone who arrived after that was moved straight to the other camps nearby, on either side."

Sonya said, "Thank you so much for the great food and for the hope that my family may be okay."

"You're very welcome, and it was nice to see you again. I hope you soon reunite with your family," Mrs. Yang said.

Sonya stood up and gave Mrs. Yang a big hug. Then she gathered up Rafe and Zola and went to find George, who had left Sonya and Mrs. Yang alone to talk. She was so excited at the prospect that Mrs. Yang had almost certainly seen her family that she could hardly contain herself. She soon found George and he could see her happiness and excitement.

He asked, "What are you looking so happy about? Good news?"

Sonya said, "I think Mrs. Yang saw my mom and my little

brother and sister. It was shortly after she got here and she said this camp was already pretty crowded. She thinks they were probably moved straight to the next camp. The next camp on my map would be the first one out of the city. If they were already here, then they had probably already passed through what my map has as the next camp. I need you to give me directions to the next camp. It must be a new one that isn't even on the map that I have."

George said, "That's great! I hope she's right. Just be prepared in case she's mistaken, okay?"

She said, "Oh, I know. But it was them. I just feel it!"

He said, "Get some rest. I will sketch up a map of the surrounding safe zones. I know where some of the newer ones are. I will make note of where most people go if they pass through this one,"

Sonya said, "Okay, thanks."

With that, Sonya, Rafe, and Zola all curled up and went to sleep. Having a renewed hope of finding her family, Sonya slept like a baby. Later on, towards evening, George returned to see if Sonya wanted something to eat. She explained that Mrs. Yang had fed her so well that she wasn't hungry and just wanted to get some more sleep. Rafe and Zola, on the other hand, were always up for something to eat. So, George made sure that they had their fill. Then the children that Rafe and Zola had been playing with before walked past and Rafe and Zola managed to get some more play time with them. When the kids went back to their families, Rafe and Zola did the same. They squeezed in on either side of Sonya and went to sleep.

In the morning, George returned with a steaming cup of

coffee. He shook Sonya to wake her and handed the cup to her. He said, "You must have been really tired. You haven't moved in almost twelve hours!"

Sonya said, "Yeah, I guess so. It's been a long journey. I'm just so glad to finally feel like I just might get to see my family soon. I've missed them so much."

George said, "I really hope you do find them. I'm sure they have missed you, too. Here's the map that I made for you. Bottom, center is where we are now. To the left is where you came from. To the right is the safe zone that your family would have most likely come through on their way here. Off the map to the bottom is the city. Anything above where we are now are the newer safe zones that opened up due to overcrowding in this one and others like it. As you can see, there is one straight up, which would be the next one people would go to after this one. From there, a road goes each way to two more on either side. Beyond that, there may be more by now, but I am not familiar with any there may be out there."

Sonya said, "Thanks. If I need more directions after this, I'm sure there will be someone who can help me with that. With any luck, this will be all I need."

George said, "I put some supplies for you over there by your pack. Would you like something to eat before you go?"

Sonya said, "I'll eat something along the way. I'm really just ready to get going. You've been a huge help. I really appreciate it."

George walked along with Sonya, Rafe, and Zola to just outside the camp to make sure she got on the right road towards her next destination. Then he wished them luck and watched them go.

# CHAPTER TWELVE

## SONYA, MEET A REAL SURPRISE

Sonya, Rafe, and Zola had been walking down a dirt road for about two hours when she realized that she wished she had taken George up on his offer to have something to eat. She stopped under a shady tree to grab a snack for herself. She also made sure Rafe and Zola had something to eat. After they had eaten, Sonya picked up a stick. Before she had even completely stood up straight, Rafe and Zola, immediately realizing that the stick meant playtime, took up their "ready" positions on either side of her. They all enjoyed a good game of fetch for about half an hour. Suddenly, playtime was interrupted by the sound of gunshots. The shots came from the direction they were heading and didn't sound like they were from very far away. Sonya got off the road to use the cover of the trees and bushes. Rafe and Zola were right there with her. They cautiously made their way to investigate, not knowing if it was friend or foe.

She had gotten used to not hearing much activity way out here, but realized that there could always be some bad guys who might have slipped out of the suburbs to spread trouble farther out while searching for supplies. About a half-mile later, she saw what looked like a couple of gang members lying dead on the road, which was still visible from where she was. She could see the pools of blood still growing so she knew this had just happened. She figured that if they were bad guys, then whoever killed them was most likely a good guy. But she couldn't see anyone else around. Sonya, Rafe, and Zola continued on, staying off the road but keeping it in sight. When a river blocked their path, they had to return to the road to walk across the bridge. When they had reached the midpoint of the bridge, a human form appeared from around the corner just beyond the bridge. They ran to the end of the bridge to try to get back into cover on the other side before they were spotted. Rafe and Zola got there first and split up to opposite sides of the road. Sonya, having seen this manoeuvre before, knew exactly what they were doing. They hadn't been spotted but this person, who looked like a soldier, spotted Sonya before she could get to cover. The soldier raised his rifle and pointed it at Sonya as he walked toward her. The soldier asked, "Who are you and what are you doing out here?"

Sonya said, "I wouldn't keep pointing that gun at me if I were you."

He said, "Answer my question."

She said, "Don't say I didn't warn you."

At that very moment, Rafe and Zola performed their signature takedown, with Zola ripping the rifle away from the man while Rafe took him to the ground with his jaws around the man's neck. Sonya, confident that this was indeed a good guy, immediately called Rafe and Zola off. Zola placed herself between the man and his rifle, making low growls, while showing her teeth, making it perfectly clear to the man that reaching for his gun would end badly. Meanwhile, Rafe stayed right in the soldier's face growling, snarling and foaming at the mouth. If the soldier had made one threatening move, Rafe would have been ready to latch back on in a millisecond! The man seemed to fully realize this since he didn't even consider going for his sidearm. Wise choice!

Although she had no intention of using it, she took the rifle from behind Zola and slowly approached the man with Zola at her side. "I told you that pointing a gun at me was a bad idea." Sonya said.

"Yeah, I see," he said.

Suddenly, Sonya realized that this man's voice was somehow familiar. As she got closer and got a look at his face, she froze in her tracks. She said, "Rafe, Zola, come."

The man said, "Sonya?"

She said, "Yeah, it's me, Dad." She started to turn and walk away.

He said, "Sonya, wait, please. Give me a chance to explain."

She asked, "Explain? What's to explain?"

He said, "I've changed. I promise. The day you drove me away, I made up my mind to get my shit together. I found help. I've been sober ever since. What you did to me, I had coming. The man I was at that time deserved it. That's when I decided that I wasn't going to be that man any more. I wanted to go back to being the man that you used to love and admire. I'd like to believe that I have done that. Now the question is whether you can find it in your heart to forgive me and let me be your dad again."

Sonya stood there, silently thinking about every word he said. She didn't say a word for several minutes while she took it all in. She remembered what Raphael had said to her. He had said, "If he was a good man once, then there is probably still a good man inside him." He had also said, "Fathers never stop loving their little girls." Sonya had been truly missing her dad's love. This was her dad, after all. He seemed totally sincere. She decided to at least talk to him some more. Finally, she said, "Okay, Dad, let's talk about it. I'm not completely sure what I'm feeling right now. But yeah, even though things got really bad between us, I do miss the dad you were, before that all happened."

He said, "Great! That's all I ask. By the way, who are your two friends?"

Sonya said, "This is Rafe and this is Zola. What are you doing here, anyway?"

He replied, "It was really a wake-up call when you beat the crap out of me and drove me away from our home. It really made me think about things. I had turned into a total asshole and didn't even realize it until that day. For you to have to do that, I was obviously deserving every bit of it. I'm glad that you did what you did. I mean, I'm sorry that you had to, but it was the only thing that made me finally straighten up. I found some people to talk to who had been through the same stuff as I had but had figured out how to cope with it. I finally got the help I needed. Once I had gotten squared away, I decided that I wanted to help people rather than hurt people. I went back to the house, once, but you had all left. I didn't know if I would ever see any of you again. So, some people I know suggested that I come out here and help out with rescuing and protecting folks being evacuated from the city. It was something constructive to do and there might be a chance of reuniting with my family if they happened to end up out here at some point. I've been doing guard duty at a couple of safe zones and patrolling the area between them ever since."

Sonya said, "I'm glad you're doing better. I hope you can stick to it, now."

He said, "There's not a doubt in my mind. I never want to go back to being that jerk again. Those are some awesome dogs you have there. How did you end up with them?"

Sonya said, "They just kinda found me, I guess."

He asked, "So, how did you end up out here? Which team rescued you and got you out?"

Sonya replied, "There was no team. It was just me, at first, until a really good friend came along. He helped me most of the way out of the city. Now it's me, Rafe, and Zola. I've been searching for Mom and the kids ever since I got out of the city."

He asked, "So, where is this friend that you mentioned?"

"He died, protecting me," she replied.

"Oh, I'm sorry," he said. Then he asked, "So, you don't know where your mother and baby brother and sister are?"

She said, "No, I had to leave without them. When you left, I had started working for a gang to make money to support the family. But I had to get away from them. It was too dangerous to try to stay and it was too dangerous to try to take them with me. So, I haven't seen them since."

He said, "Well, I've been going back and forth between the safe zone about a half-mile up this road and the next one beyond that. They aren't in either of these two places."

Sonya said, "I've visited every safe zone back that way, on my way here, and they weren't there."

He said, "Then the best bet would be some of the newer safe zones up north. Let's go to the one I've been calling home lately, get some rest and supplies. I'll find someone to take my place out here, and we can head north tomorrow."

"We?" Sonya asked.

He said, "Yeah, I was hoping we could look for them

together. I'd like for us to be a family again. That is, if you'll allow me to be part of your life again."

Sonya said, "Let's go to the safe zone, get some rest and supplies, and then I will have to think about the rest for a while. We can talk some more along the way."

"Fair enough," he said.

As they walked along, he had so many questions for her. He wanted to know more about how Sonya had made it out. He wanted to know more about the people who had helped her along the way. She told him about how she had met Raphael and all about the adventures they had together. She told him about the things Raphael had told her and just what a great person he was. She used the story about his Zola and how he had risked his life trying to find her to illustrate what a loyal friend he was. She explained that this was how Rafe and Zola got their names. Some of the things she told her dad about Raphael made him smile and laugh. Others had him welling up with tears. He said that he wished he could have met Raphael. When they reached the safe zone, Sonya and her dad sat down to rest and have something to eat. She continued to tell him all about everyone she had encountered during her travels. Rafe and Zola were doing the "puppy dog eyes" thing while they were eating. He gave them each a little of what he was having and Sonya said, "That's how it starts!"

He said, "That's how what starts?"

As Rafe and Zola began licking his face, Sonya said, "That!"

At that moment, he lost his balance and fell off the stool he was sitting on. He was now on his back, on the ground, with Rafe and Zola on top of him, slobbering all over his face.

Sonya started laughing uncontrollably at her dad's

predicament. She said, "It seems like they're okay with you."

He said, "Aren't you gonna call them off?"

She said, "Nope, not this time. This is too much fun!" Finally, though, she did call them off. He said, while wiping all the slobber off his face, "So, if they're okay with me, how about you?"

She said, "They're pretty good judges of character, so, yeah, we can be family again."

He said, "I won't ever let you down again. I promise. Thank you, Sonya. Let me find my replacement for tomorrow and then we can get some rest. We'll head out in the morning, okay?"

"Roger that," Sonya said.

He said, "Haven't heard that in way too long. I really missed you, Sonya. I won't ever let anything come between us again. I lost you once. Never again."

He went off to find someone to take over his patrol duties. When he returned, he had another soldier with him. He said, "This is a friend of mine. He's got a lot to do with getting me back on the straight and narrow. He wanted to meet you. Kent, this is my daughter, Sonya. Sonya, this is Kent."

Sonya said, "Nice to meet you, Kent. Thank you for getting my dad back to being my dad."

Kent said, "Nice to meet you, Sonya. Your dad has told me a lot about you. And for the record, your dad never stopped being your dad for a second. He talked about you all the time. He just lost his way for a bit. Lots of us have gone through the same thing. It's not always easy to transition back to civilized life after some of the things we had to do. Some find it harder than others. Some don't ever make it back at all. But your dad is back, one hundred percent. He's been a lot of help here and we will definitely miss him. But he has a new mission now. So, you take good care of him, okay?"

"Yep, I sure will. Thanks again for helping him out," Sonya said.

"That's what we do. Never leave a brother behind," Kent said.

As Kent walked away, Sonya looked at her dad and said, "I'm glad you had such a great friend as Kent to help you. You're so stubborn that I'm surprised you let him."

He said, "It just so happens that Kent was just a little more stubborn than me! He simply would not give up on me. He kept reminding me of what a great family I had and that my only chance of getting that back was to get sober and live my life right. I'm not sure if I'd even be alive right now if not for his help. I owe him a lot. You and I would definitely not be talking right now if not for him."

Sonya said, "Yeah, that's for sure. I had pretty much decided that I no longer had a father. Did that hurt? Sure. But the person you had turned into was not someone I wanted to be any part of my life."

He said, "I totally get it. You were absolutely right to get me away from your mom. I might have hurt her really bad, or even worse. I just hope that if we find her, she can forgive me."

Sonya said, "Not 'if'; *when* we find her. We are going to find her. I just know it."

He said, "Roger that."

She smiled the biggest smile she had for a long time and said, "Well, what are we waiting for? Let's do this!"

He said, "First, a good night's sleep, then first thing in the morning, we go, okay?"

Sonya gave her dad a thumbs up and another big smile. Then she settled back to get some sleep. Rafe curled up next to her but Zola went and curled up next to her dad. Sonya gave him a wink and said, "Good night, Dad."

He said, "Good night, Sonya." He was still giving Zola a belly rub as he eventually drifted off to sleep.

# CHAPTER THIRTEEN

## SONYA, MEET YOUR TRUE DAD

When morning arrived, Sonya was greeted by a cup of coffee and a plate of breakfast which her dad had brought to her. He said, "Good morning, daughter."

She said, "Good morning, Dad. Thanks, I'm starved."

He said, "I knew you would be. When you were little, you always woke me up way before I wanted to get up to make you breakfast. You'd always say, 'I'm starved', just like you said, just now."

"Really?" Sonya asked.

"Yep," he said.

They both had a laugh at how some things, apparently, hadn't changed. As they were eating their breakfast, he pulled out a map of the safe zones they would be traveling to. He explained how Kent had made this map for them while they were asleep. Just then, Kent walked over to where they were.

Kent said, "Good morning, you two. I'm so glad to see you two back together as family, again. Are you all ready to go find the rest of the family?"

Sonya said, "Yes, thanks to you. I can't find words to tell you how much I appreciate all you have done."

Sonya's dad said, "We'll be heading out in just a few minutes. Kent, I don't know how I can thank you enough for getting me to this moment in my life. I have my daughter back, thanks to you. This is something I didn't know if I would ever experience again. Thanks, brother!"

Kent said, "Don't mention it. I'm just so happy for both of you. Safe travels, both of you. Maybe we'll catch each other again someday, downrange."

Sonya's dad and Kent shook hands and gave each other a salute. Kent reached to shake Sonya's hand but Sonya, being Sonya, went in for the hug saying, "Thank you."

He replied, "You're welcome. Take good care of him, okay?"

"Got it," she said.

As Kent walked away, Sonya started stowing her supplies into her pack and her dad was doing the same. Then they shouldered their packs and with Rafe and Zola at their sides, they started their journey together as father and daughter, reunited. On their way out of the camp, they thanked everyone who had been so kind and hospitable to them.

They had about a seven-mile hike to the first place they were heading to. This gave them plenty of time to talk. Sonya shared many more tales of all that she had been through. He also told her what had been going on in his life both before and after the time when he finally decided to get sober. This allowed her to understand what kind of demons he had been dealing with. He had never told her about some of the horrible things he had done and seen when he was on deployments. But, now that she was older, he felt she could handle it. He figured that she should know what drove him to the brink. He wanted her to understand that it was not that he just decided one day to turn into a monster. The monster grew inside him from what he had experienced. For a while, the monster took him over. It was something he couldn't control on his own.

Only after she sent him packing did he finally admit he needed help to control the monster. With that help, he eventually regained control.

Sonya said, "I had no idea how bad it had become for you. Now I get it. It was never your fault. No one should be forced to do the kinds of things you were forced to do. No one should have to see the things you saw. I'm so sorry you had to go through all of those awful experiences. I'm just glad that you are back to being you again."

He said, "I'm glad you understand. Thank you, Sonya. Now, I've spilled my guts. So, how about telling me a little more about what you've been through? Talking really does help. It'll make you feel better almost immediately. For instance, what about this friend, Raphael? You have told me so little. I mean, were you two… uh… um, well, you know?"

Sonya said, "What, like boyfriend and girlfriend? No. Hell no!"

He said, "It's just that you seem to miss him so badly and you speak so highly of him that I thought maybe, just maybe…"

"No. No way," she said. She went on, "It was never like that. He had just been such an awesome friend to me in the short time we knew each other. We were so connected. We could almost read each other's minds. He was like the big brother I never had. He was always looking out for me. In the end, he gave his life to save mine."

He said, "Well, then he has my eternal thanks. I wish he was here so I could tell him myself. I'm sorry he died, Sonya. But I'm so glad that he saved you."

Sonya stopped walking, turned to her dad, and gave him a big hug, saying, "I've really missed you, Dad. I love you."

He said, “I love you, too, Sonya,” as he wiped a tear from his eye.

Sonya asked, “Are you crying?”

He said, “Uh… no, just some dust in my eye.”

She said, “Yeah, right!”

They both laughed at how mushy they had just been, then continued on down the road. With about three miles to go to their destination, suddenly they were startled by the sound of something crashing through the brush behind them. As they spun around to look, two deer ran past them, narrowly missing them.

“What the hell?” Sonya said.

Her dad said, “Find some cover. Something spooked those deer. I have my rifle, so I will go check it out. I need you to be safe while I do that.”

Sonya ducked down behind some bushes off the side of the road while her dad, with his rifle up and ready, slowly moved towards the area the deer had come crashing out of. Meanwhile, of their own accord, Rafe and Zola were trailing just behind him, one on each side of the road, just in the bushes, out of sight, but keeping their eyes glued to him and staying within striking distance should their assistance be required. Sonya watched in amazement at how well they worked as a team. She couldn’t help but notice that watching “her kids” in action was making her feel a sense of pride. He was about a hundred yards down the road when a man came running out of the brush with his gun pointed at her dad. He was telling the man to lower his weapon or he would be forced to shoot. With his attention focused on the man in front of him, he had no idea that there was now a man coming out of the bushes from the opposite side of the road behind him. This man had a gun pointed right at his head and was slowly coming up from behind to within thirty yards. Sonya watched this all in horror from where she was, unable to do anything to help. The man in front of him was not complying with his order to lower his weapon and he was preparing to shoot the man. At that very second, Rafe and Zola were airborne on their final approach to the other man. He pulled the trigger to kill the man in front of him and at the exact same time, he heard the commotion behind him. When he turned around, he saw Rafe and Zola making quick work of the other man that he had no idea was seconds from killing him. Sonya was now running to get to where her dad, Rafe, and Zola were. By the time she got there, all three were rolling around together in a mass of licks, kisses, and belly rubs. He knew that he would have been dead if not for these two brave, powerful, loving dogs. Sonya joined in to show her two heroes how much their actions were appreciated.

He said, "If it wasn't for these two, I'd be a goner!"

Sonya said, "Yeah, they are really something, aren't they?

They went a little ways up the road and decided to take a break. Sonya and her dad were showing Rafe and Zola all of the love and affection they so richly deserved. There were plenty of treats given and a little game of fetch between Rafe, Zola, and Dad. Sonya just sat and watched, enjoying every minute of the fun they were obviously having. It was almost perfect. The only thing that could make this scene complete would be to have the rest of her family present. She hoped that this would be the case very soon.

Once playtime was over, the four of them, once again, started hiking towards the safe zone which was now about two miles ahead.

# CHAPTER FOURTEEN

## SONYA, MEET YOUR FAMILY

As they neared the safe zone, they were greeted by two soldiers who were patrolling the road leading to the safe zone, as was the case for all of these areas. When they saw Sonya's dad, they simply gave a quick salute and let them pass.

Sonya asked, "You know them?"

He replied, "No, but they obviously could tell we're on the good side."

She said, "Yeah, guess so, huh."

They walked into the camp with high hopes of finding the rest of their family. Sonya was excited and anxious at the same time. There were a lot of people here and it would take some time to have a look at everyone. As eager as they were to begin investigating, there wasn't much day left and they were all tired from the adventures of the day.

A man approached them with an outstretched hand. As he shook hands with Sonya's dad, he said, "I'm Paul. Welcome!"

Sonya's dad said, "Thank you. I'm Clint. This is my daughter, Sonya. And these two are Rafe and Zola."

Paul said, "Nice to meet all of you. What brings you to our camp?"

Sonya said, "We're looking for my mom and little brother and sister."

Clint said, "Sonya has been to almost every safe zone on

this side of the city. I'm familiar with the ones around here. With neither of us having any luck finding them, this was the next logical place for them to possibly be. So, here we are."

Paul said, "Well, you're welcome to have a look around and stay as long as you like. In the morning, I could show you around. But right now, I have to go tuck in my little ones."

Clint said, "We're about ready to crash, ourselves. We had a pretty long day."

Paul led them to a place where they could spend the night. They thanked him and he went off to be with his family. Sonya and her dad had a little something to eat, while also making sure Rafe and Zola had something to eat, and then made themselves comfortable for a good night's sleep. Rafe and Zola also made themselves comfortable by practically squishing Sonya and her dad.

Sonya asked, "Dad, do you think Mom is here?"

He replied, "I don't know. I feel like we are getting really close to finding her, though. We're on the right track. If not here, we will find her, maybe at the next place. It won't be much longer. I feel it."

Sonya said, "I sure hope you're right. I really miss her."

"I know you do. I miss her too," he said. "Now, try to get some sleep."

"I love you, Dad," she said.

He said, "I love you too. Good night."

"Good night," she said.

In the morning, Paul showed up carrying two cups of coffee. "Good morning," he said.

Taking one of the cups of coffee, Sonya said, "Thank you. Good morning."

Clint said, “Good morning. Thanks, but no. I never touch the stuff.”

Paul said, “Gee, I had my coffee already. Seems a shame it’ll go to waste.”

Sonya said, “Whoa, hold up, there. It won’t go to waste. You can set that down right here!” Paul and Clint looked at each other and chuckled.

Sonya said, “What can I say? I love coffee!”

Paul said, “Why don’t you two come and join me and my wife for some breakfast? She made plenty.”

“Okay,” they both said in unison.

Paul led them to a tent a short distance away. He held the flap open for them to enter, following them in. He said, “Clint, Sonya, this is my wife, Grace. Grace, meet Clint and his daughter, Sonya.”

Grace said, “Hello and welcome. It’s nice to meet both of you.”

Sonya said, “Nice to meet you, too.”

Clint said, “Yeah, nice to meet you. Thank you for your hospitality.”

Grace said, “Well, don’t be shy. Dig in!”

Sonya said, “You don’t have to ask me twice. This looks fantastic and I’m starved!”

Clint said, “Yeah, what she said!”

Grace said, “The kids already ate and went off to play. So, help yourselves to all you want.”

They all ate their fill and Grace, noticing that Rafe and Zola were sitting there looking as if they felt left out, made sure they got something to eat, as well.

Sonya said, “Thank you. That was really good. And thanks for feeding Rafe and Zola, too. You didn’t have to.”

Grace said, "Are you kidding? I couldn't see them go without. I've always loved dogs. Besides, they remind me of a dog I had when I was little."

Paul said, "Well, if you are ready, I can show you around. Let's see if we can't get this family whole again!"

Sonya said, "Yeah, let's go!"

As they started to slowly and methodically make their way through the camp, they talked as they walked along. Paul was making sure they were able to get a look at everyone along the way. Occasionally, he would stop and introduce them to people they encountered. He would explain that Sonya and Clint were searching for their family and have Sonya describe her mom and siblings in order to see if anyone might think they had seen them.

Paul said, "It's amazing to me just how large this place has gotten. I'm actually not sure if we can cover it all in one day. Ya know, before all of this happened, and we all lived in the city, we knew there were a lot of people. But when all of these people have to relocate, that's when you truly realize just how many people there really are. It's not just here, either. How many other safe zones are there? Dozens? Hundreds? Heck, I don't know. But I'm sure they are all growing all of the time. And when they run out of room, new ones open up. And it just goes on and on and on. It's a shame things got the way they are. The cities are unliveable thanks to the fact that the gangs completely took over. But now that I've been out here for a while, I'm no longer sure if it's a curse or a blessing. I'm actually starting to like it out here."

Sonya said, "It's funny that you say that. I kinda feel the same way. The first night I spent out here on my own was the first time I truly saw the night sky. It was the first time I experienced actual quiet, broken only by the sounds of nature. It was absolutely beautiful. And it's where I met these two. Now that Rafe and Zola are with me, I can't imagine life without them."

Clint said, "I'm not sure I would go back even if things did get back to normal."

Sonya said, "I know I wouldn't. I had decided that after that first night out here. Out here is where I plan to spend the rest of my days, with my family, hopefully."

They continued moving through the camp until about midday with no sign of Sonya's mom or siblings. No one they had described them to seemed to have any recollection of seeing them, either. Sonya was looking a little discouraged. Paul suggested that they should take a break and have something to eat. He tried to reassure Sonya by telling her that they hadn't even covered half of the camp yet so there were still many people to see.

Sonya said, "It's just been such a long, hard journey to get to this point. It's starting to wear on me a bit."

Her dad said, "You have to stay strong, Sonya. The long hard journey to get here is exactly why you can't give up hope, now."

Paul said, "You're going to find them. You have to keep believing that, okay?"

Sonya said, "Yeah, you're right. Let's keep going."

As they were walking along, suddenly, Rafe and Zola froze in their tracks and were vigorously sniffing as if they smelled something they recognized. They paced back and forth, constantly sniffing as if to zero in on the source of what they were smelling. Then, without warning, they both bolted off in the direction upwind of where they all were.

Paul said, "What's that about? Where are they going?"

Clint said, "I don't know, but whatever they smelled sure got their attention."

Sonya said, "C'mon, let's go! Whatever it is, it's something they must recognize."

Paul said, "They know the scent of you two. You don't suppose…"

Before Paul could finish his sentence, Rafe and Zola were sitting on either side of a little boy and a little girl. As Paul was about to suggest, Rafe and Zola had picked up a familiar scent, alright. It was familiar because it was the same scent as Sonya's and her dad's. It was Sonya's little brother and sister! Sonya ran to them with open arms.

They said, "Sonya?"

She said, "Yes, it's me! Oh, Samuel and Hannah, I'm so glad to see you guys! Thank God you're okay!"

Clint had also run over to where the rest of his children were, and a group hug was taking place. It was such a joyful reunion. Paul stood back and let them have their moment. Paul knew about Samuel and Hannah and he knew something that was going to make the reunion bitter sweet. He was welling up with tears, knowing that in a matter of seconds, the mood was going to change drastically.

Sonya asked Samuel and Hannah, "Where's Mom?"

They both started to cry. Clint fell to his knees knowing that something horrible must have happened.

Sonya asked, "What? What is it? What happened?" Sonya was now crying, knowing that something bad must have happened to her mom.

Paul walked over and said, "I'm so sorry. If I had known

that Samuel and Hannah were your brother and sister, Sonya, and your children, Clint, I would have told you, already. Sonya, shortly after your mom got here, she started to get very sick. The only person here with any medical training is a nurse named Kathy who helped a lot of people in the hospital she worked at in the city. She had worked with a lot of people who had Covid and was sure your mom had it. But unfortunately, we don't have the kind of equipment here that is needed to treat Covid. So, all she could do was to make her as comfortable as possible. She fought hard. Your mom wrote a letter to you and insisted that Kathy hold onto it to give to you if you ever came through here. I will find Kathy and send her over to speak with you. Again, I am truly, so very sorry."

With that, Paul went to find Kathy. The four of them cried and hugged and cried some more. There were no words to describe the happiness of finding Samuel and Hannah, while at the same time dealing with the loss of Sonya's mom. Sonya was dealing with another emotion, as well.

Guilt. She felt as if she had denied her dad the chance to be with her mom when she needed him most.

She said, "Dad, I'm so s…"

He said, "No, Sonya, you have nothing to say you're sorry for. You did what you knew was best at the time. And you were absolutely right. No one knew this would happen. It's not your fault, so don't you dare blame yourself for it."

"But I feel so bad that you couldn't be there for her," Sonya said, crying.

He said, "And I could say that I feel bad that you weren't with her. That was my fault. My behavior was what brought all of this about. So, I am the one who should be sorry. And believe me, I am."

Then they hugged and cried together as they pulled Samuel and Hannah into the hug with them.

Then they noticed a woman standing nearby. There was another woman and a man standing directly behind her.

Clint said, "You must be Kathy."

She said, "Yes, and I want you to meet Mary and Ron. They've been looking after Hannah and Samuel. They've treated them just as they would treat their own children. If you wouldn't have made it back to Hannah and Samuel, they would have continued to raise them as their own."

Mary said, "But we're so happy to see you reunited with them."

Ron said, "And we're so sorry for your loss."

Sonya said, "Thank you so much for taking care of them."

Mary and Ron knelt down to hug Hannah and Samuel one last time and to say goodbye to them.

Then Mary started to cry and walked away. Ron followed, trying to comfort her.

Clint quickly caught up to them and with one hand on each of their shoulders, said, "Thank you both so much."

Kathy then said, "Sonya, your mom wrote this and made me promise that if I ever saw you, I would give it to you. She was such a sweet woman. I wish I could have done more for her."

Sonya said, "You did what you could and I thank you for that."

Clint had returned and said, "Yes, Kathy, thank you for taking care of her the best you could."

Sonya opened the envelope and removed the letter inside. Through her tears, she struggled to read it. By the time she had reached the end, she was weeping uncontrollably. She passed it to her dad to let him read it. It said:

'My dearest Sonya, I hope and pray that one day you will be able to read this. That will mean that you have made it out safely. Just a few days after you left, some good people led us out of the city. We were moved from one camp to another until we ended up here. Shortly after that, I started to feel sick. A nice couple is taking care of Hannah and Samuel. Their names are Mary and Ron. I'm not going to make it much longer. I just can't seem to breathe. I hope someday you will be back together with your little brother and sister. They miss you terribly. And I beg you to forgive your father. He is a good man. He was just having a really difficult time dealing with things he saw and did while serving our country. I don't know if you will ever see him again, but if you do, give him a chance. He loves you. Heaven, for me, would be knowing that you and your father have reunited. I love you, Sonya. I will be at peace soon. My wish is that you can live a peaceful life for all of your days. God bless you, daughter. Love, Mom.'

Clint was sobbing by the time he had finished reading.

Sonya wrapped her arms around her dad and said, "I don't know how to live without her, Dad."

Clint said, "Your mom had five wishes, according to her letter. Four have already happened. How you live without her is to grant her fifth wish. She is already smiling down on us from Heaven. Let's make her smile even bigger."

"How?" Sonya asked.

He replied, "We find someplace to live our lives peacefully. We're going to find a new home where Hannah, Samuel, you and I can live, peacefully."

Kathy had walked a short distance away to give them some privacy. They walked over to where she was. They once again thanked her for all she had done. Then they asked her where Sonya's mom had been buried.

Kathy said, "Oh, we didn't bury her. We cremated her. I have her urn in my tent. I've been keeping her remains safe so that if this day came, I could give them to you."

Sonya said, "Oh, thank you. It will be nice to be able to take her along with us. Wherever we end up calling home will be her home, too." Sonya was now starting to cry all over again.

Clint said, "Thank you for this, Kathy. This really means a lot to all of us."

Kathy said, "You're all so very welcome. It was the least I could do."

Kathy went to her tent and came back with the urn. She handed it to Clint. He knelt down amongst his children and they all placed their hands on the urn.

Hannah asked, "Is this Mom?"

Sonya, alternately touching Hannah's chest, then Samuel's chest, then her own chest said, "No, Mom is here."

Clint, touching his own chest, said, "And here. This urn is only what is left of her physical body. Everything that made your mom 'Mom' lives on inside all of us whenever we think of her."

Kathy, wiping a tear from her eye, said, "Amen."

Clint said, "It's been a difficult day. We're all going to be tired tonight. We would like to rest here for the night and, in the morning, I think we'd like to go and start looking for someplace to call home. Kathy, do you have any suggestions for how we might go about doing that?"

Kathy replied, "The camp we are in is one of the farthest from the city. So, as you go farther out in that direction, there is open country, fields, and farms. I have no clue what you might find out there. I've never ventured out that far. All you can do is look around and ask people questions."

Clint said, "Well then, I guess that's what we'll do."

Kathy asked, "You will stick around for breakfast, won't you?"

Sonya said, "Absolutely!"

Kathy said, "Good! I will see you in the morning, then." As Kathy walked away, they were all sitting there in quiet thought. It was time to reflect on the loss of their wife and mother. Hannah and Samuel were sound asleep in just a few minutes.

Sonya and her dad picked them up and moved them to someplace more comfortable, covering them up with blankets and kissing them goodnight on their foreheads.

Sonya said, "How can they sleep so easily knowing Mom is gone?"

Clint said, "For one, they've known about it for a while, already. Second, they're little. Little kids grieve much differently than we do. They just don't, at that age, fully realize what death really is."

Sonya asked, "What do you think we will find out there tomorrow?"

Clint said, "I don't know. But I do know that whatever we find, we will find it together. And for that, I am truly thankful."

"Me too, Dad," Sonya said, as she struggled to keep her eyes open.

Clint walked over, put a blanket over Sonya, and kissed her forehead, saying, "Good night, Sonya. I love you."

# CHAPTER FIFTEEN

## SONYA, MEET YOUR NEW HOME

When morning arrived, Kathy had breakfast prepared for Sonya, Clint, Hannah, and Samuel.

When they had finished, they said goodbye to Kathy, thanking her again for all she had done. They also asked her to give their gratitude to Mary and Ron, agreeing that it might be too painful for all involved to thank them in person. They started to walk away, but Sonya turned around and ran back to Kathy for one last hug.

Kathy said, "You all take care of yourselves, okay?"

Sonya said, "We will. Thanks for everything."

Kathy said, "Oh, wait, I almost forgot. I have some going away gifts for all of you. I found these bivy tents which we have no use for. They may come in handy for you during your travels. Who knows how many nights it may be before you find something more permanent for shelter."

Sonya said, "Thank you! That's so thoughtful of you."

Sonya gave Kathy another hug and then re-joined her family. They started walking down the road leading out of the camp and farther out into the countryside. They were looking forward to seeing what they might find as they got farther from all of the troubles they were leaving behind.

Hannah and Samuel quickly realized how much Rafe and Zola loved to play. As they were walking along, they passed the time throwing sticks ahead of them for the dogs to retrieve. This game never got old and it kept the kids occupied. This gave Sonya and her dad a chance to do a lot of catching up. He wanted to know more about all of the adventures she had experienced during her journey. The more he heard, the more impressed he was at her ability to handle almost any situation. By midday, she had told him pretty much everything that had happened while he was away. Sonya had managed to coax her dad into telling more of his story as well. The conversation was very therapeutic for both of them.

They stopped to have a snack and to rest a bit. They had covered about five miles and Sonya knew that Hannah and Samuel were probably a little tired. It was a lot of walking for little kids. After they had rested a bit, they decided to get moving again. Sonya and her dad picked up the little ones to let them piggyback ride for a while. About three more miles down the road, they came upon a small lake with clear water and a sandy shoreline. It was obvious that those tents Kathy had given them were going to immediately come in handy. They set up the tents on the shore and before they had finished, Rafe and Zola were already enjoying the water. Sonya's dad began gathering wood for a campfire and Sonya asked Hannah and Samuel if they wanted to have a swim. Sonya went in first and discovered that the bottom was smooth and the water was shallow for a long way out. Once satisfied that it was a good safe place for the kids, she told them to join her.

Rafe, Zola, Hannah, Samuel, and Sonya were all playing, splashing, and having a great time. Clint had finished gathering wood and a small campfire was now crackling.

Sonya said, "C'mon, Dad! The water's great. Jump in!"

Clint said, "Oh, I don't know."

It melted his heart when Hannah and Samuel said, "Yeah, c'mon, Dad!"

He said, "Okay, it looks like too much fun for me to pass up."

The six of them were having a ball! They splashed and laughed and had a fantastic time. They were truly together as a real family, again. After nearly two hours, they got out and dried off by the fire and had something to eat. They were all having a hard time keeping their eyes open so they got into the tents and were sound asleep in minutes.

In the morning, Sonya was awakened by the smell of coffee brewing over the campfire. Clint had woken up about an hour earlier and knew how much Sonya would appreciate some coffee first thing in the morning.

Sonya asked, "Coffee? Is that coffee I smell or am I dreaming? Where in the world did you get coffee?"

Clint replied, "Paul sent some along since he knows how much you love the stuff."

Sonya said, "That was very thoughtful of him."

Clint handed her a steaming cup and said, "Here you go. Enjoy. Now, I'm going to fix us some breakfast. We'll wait to wake Hannah and Samuel until it's ready. They're pretty tired and need their rest. We've got a long hike ahead of us again today."

Sonya said, "Thanks, Dad,"

Clint went about making breakfast while Sonya sipped her coffee. She couldn't help but smile, thinking about just how happy she was to have her dad in her life again. He let her know when breakfast was nearly ready and she went to wake up Hannah and Samuel. They all sat around the fire and enjoyed their meal, and also just enjoyed being together.

When they had finished eating and Sonya had finished her third cup of coffee, they packed up the tents, gathered their belongings, and prepared for the day's journey. Then they got back on the road and leisurely walked along. There didn't seem to be any hurry. They were all so content just being on this adventure together. As had become routine, Rafe and Zola were in the lead with Hannah and Samuel right behind, throwing sticks for the dogs to retrieve, generally having a great time. Sonya and Clint brought up the rear, continuing to talk about everything that had happened in their lives while they were out of contact with each other. They only managed to cover about five miles by the time it was midday. They stopped to have a snack and rest for a bit.

After about forty-five minutes, they decided it was time to get moving again. They needed to put a few more miles behind them, as well as find a good spot to spend the night. They had walked for about two more hours and gone only about three more miles. The slow pace was dictated by the fact that Hannah and Samuel really couldn't be expected to go much faster. There wasn't really any need to be in a hurry, anyway. They were now almost thirty miles away from the city and there was no sign of trouble out here. It was downright peaceful. As they crested a hill, they could see what appeared to be a well-maintained farm in the valley about a mile up the road.

As they got closer to the farm, they noticed a man working on a fence next to the road. Sonya approached the man trying her best not to startle him. She said, "Hello, sir. Beautiful day and a beautiful farm you have here."

He replied, "Hello. Thank you. We sure like it."

She said, "We are just passing through. We left the city to get away from all of the violence that's happening there. We are looking for someplace to call home. That's my dad, Clint. Those two are Hannah and Samuel, my little sister and brother. Those other two are Rafe and Zola. And my name is Sonya. Do you know if there is any place where we can make a new home around here?"

He replied, "My name is Pete. Pleasure to meet all of you. I'm just a hired hand, here. You would have to ask Mr. and Mrs. Greene. They own this place. They may be able to answer your question. They should be up by the house. Just follow the road a little farther and you can't miss it."

Clint said, "Okay, thanks. Nice meeting you."

As they walked toward the farm house, Sonya asked, "Dad, we don't have any money, so even if we find a place to call home, how will we pay for it?"

He replied, "I don't know. I figured I would worry about that if we actually found a place. We will figure something out when the time comes."

They were about a hundred yards from the house when they came upon a man who was working on a tractor with his back towards them. Sonya walked up behind him and asked, "Are you Mr. Greene?"

Startled, he turned towards her saying, "Hello?"

She exclaimed, "Frank!"

He said, "Sonya! How are you?"

Sonya said, "I'm fine. It's so good to see you. But I thought you weren't going to leave your house, no matter what. What are you doing here?"

Frank replied, "My family finally convinced me to get out of the suburb. So, here I am. This is their farm. Where's Raphael?"

"He didn't make it," she said, wiping a tear from her eye.

"Oh, Sonya, I am so very sorry. He was a great guy. I really liked him," Frank said.

"Yeah, I sure miss him," Sonya said. "He was a true friend. I want to introduce you to my family. This is my dad, Clint. Over there are my little brother and sister, Samuel and Hannah. The two they are playing with are Rafe and Zola."

"Glad to meet you, Clint," he said as he reached out to shake Clint's hand. "Sonya, I could have sworn you were looking for your little brother, sister, and mother. I don't recall you mentioning your dad."

Sonya replied, "My mom passed away after she had made it safely out of the city."

"Oh my! Again, I am so sorry, Sonya," Frank said.

Sonya said, "Thanks. I hadn't mentioned my dad because at that time, he wasn't in my life. But we recently reunited. Then we found Hannah and Samuel. The loss of my mom really hurts but having the rest of us all together as a family again makes it a little easier."

Suddenly, their conversation was interrupted by a commotion and a blur of fur passing them at warp speed. It was Rafe and Zola accompanied by two more dogs chasing them around in circles and play fighting, all having a great time.

Frank said, "Looks like your dogs and our dogs have introduced themselves."

Sonya said, "Yep. And it looks like they are having a great time."

"You said their names are Rafe and Zola, right?" Frank asked. "How did you come to have two dogs? You didn't have dogs before. Wait a minute. Rafe? Named after Raphael?"

Sonya said, "Yes, and Zola was the name of his dog that he had before I met him. So, when these two dogs entered my life, I wanted to honor the memory of Raphael and his dog by naming them after him and his Zola."

Frank said, "They are beautiful dogs."

Sonya said, "They saved my life more than once."

"Mine too," Clint said.

Frank asked, "So, what's next for all of you?"

Clint said, "We're hoping to find someplace peaceful to call home."

"Come with me. I think my sister and brother-in-law just might be able to help you with that. I'll introduce you to them and I'll even put in a good word for you," Frank said with a wink.

They couldn't imagine just what he meant by that. They looked at one another with puzzlement on their faces. He led them to the back side of the house where there were two people working in a huge vegetable garden.

He said, "Joan, Kevin, I have some folks I would like you to meet. Remember when I told you about the kids who stayed with me for a couple days? Well, this is one of them, Sonya. And, this is her dad, Clint. Those are her brother and sister, Samuel and Hannah, playing with the dogs over there. Sonya and Clint, meet Joan and Kevin Greene. These good people are looking for a place to call home. I told them that you might be able to help them out with that." Then he smiled and winked at Joan and Kevin, saying, "I've still got a lot of work to do so I will leave all of you to talk." With that, he started to walk back to the tractor he had been working on, winking again at Sonya and Clint as he passed them.

Sonya said, "Mrs. Greene, Mr. Greene, it's a pleasure to

meet you."

"Oh, please just call us Joan and Kevin," Joan said, "We're all friends here. If you're a friend of Frank's, you're a friend of ours."

Clint said, "Well, it's good to meet you. Quite a place you have here. It's so peaceful. It's just like what we are hoping to find, someday, to call home."

"Yeah, Frank said you might be able to help us with finding a place to call home. Do you know of someplace that might work for us?" Sonya asked.

Joan, giving a wink to Kevin, said, "Yeah, I think we just might."

Kevin said, "Let's go for a little walk. We can talk along the way."

Joan and Kevin led them across the yard to the beginning of a footpath which disappeared into the woods. Kevin explained that it was about a ten-minute walk to where they were heading and that it would give them time to get to know each other a little better.

Joan said, "Clint, it looks like you might be in the military?"

He said, "That's right. Lately, I've been helping to try to keep the bad stuff that's been going on in the city from spreading to places like this. I spent some time working security for some of the safe zone camps where people who have been evacuated from the city are living."

Joan said, "Sonya, I have to say, Frank has told us all about you. He thinks the world of you. He thought the world of your friend Raphael, too. Where is he now?"

"He died protecting me just before I made it out of the city," Sonya replied.

"I'm sorry," Joan said, "I wish he could have made it out. Frank would have loved seeing him again. Frank is sure happy to see you, though. His face hasn't lit up like that for a long, long time. He said that even though he only got to spend a couple days getting to know you, he was really impressed with you. He said that if he would have had a daughter, he would want her to be just like you."

"He said that?" Sonya asked.

Joan said, "He sure did. He was so glad to have company for those couple days. After his wife passed away, he was all alone for a long time. He gave the appearance that he was handling it okay, but he was actually a lot more lonely than he would admit. He said he would have loved it if you two could have stayed longer but he knew you couldn't."

"He is such a sweet man," Sonya said. "I cried when we left him. I wished we could have stayed longer, too."

Clint asked, "I can't handle the curiosity any longer. Where, exactly, are you taking us?"

Kevin said, "Since we have a little way to go, still, let me explain why the place we're heading to exists in the first place. Bordering our land, there is a huge nature preserve. People from the city used to visit it, just to experience the outdoors and nature. You know, just to get away from the hustle and bustle and noise of the city. As they were heading to and from this place, they would occasionally stop here and ask where the nearest accommodations were. They would say that they wanted to spend more than one day out here at a time so they needed somewhere to spend the night. At that time, all we could do was to send them back to the hotels and motels closer to the suburbs.

One day, the lightbulb finally came on for us. We built four little cabins to rent out to these folks so they wouldn't have to go so far to spend the night. By the end of the first summer, we were regularly filling all four and still turning people away. We put up four more cabins and still had to turn people away sometimes. Word of our cabins had spread and eventually we ended up with twenty cabins. We would probably have had even more, but we ran out of space. It was a nice little side business for us. People would stay here for the weekend or sometimes for the whole week. They really enjoyed the break from city life and the nature preserve offered enough hiking trails to keep them exploring and entertained for days. Then, as another benefit, they would always buy some fresh produce from us. They would rave about how much better it was than anything they could buy in a grocery store.

So, now here we are. We have twenty cabins and with all that has been going on, there aren't any people coming to stay in them. We still have a huge garden and fruit trees and nobody to eat it all. We still have livestock and chickens but there aren't places to sell any of that any more, either."

Joan said, "What he is trying to say is if you folks need a place to stay, you're looking at it."

At that very second, they rounded a curve in the trail and stepped into a large opening in the woods. In this opening were the twenty cabins which Kevin had just spoken of. A few of them showed signs that people were living in them. Joan explained that those were people who lived there in exchange for helping out around the farm. The rest were obviously vacant.

Kevin said, "Take your pick. Any vacant cabin is your new home if you want it to be."

Sonya said, "No way, you're kidding, right?"

"We really can't. We have no way to pay you. It wouldn't be right," Clint said.

"Pay? You don't need to pay," Joan said. "There's always something we could use a hand with around here. If you're willing to help with chores and stuff, you've got a home. Besides, it's a shame to have these cabins sitting empty. They're really quite comfortable. I've actually tried them out myself a few times just for fun. Best sleep you'll ever get, I promise."

Kevin said, "We insist. Please stay."

Sonya, looking first at her dad, then back to Joan and Kevin, said, "Maybe we can stay for a while, at least. You know, until we think of something else."

To which Clint added, "Yeah, maybe just temporarily. My background could come in handy too, if trouble ever shows up out here. We really appreciate your offer. We'll stay for now."
Frank had come up the path and was standing behind them at this point. He said, "Great! We can be neighbors!"

Joan said, "Well, it's settled then. Make yourselves at home. We're going to barbecue later, so once you're settled in, come back down to the house and join us. We have plenty of food."

They enjoyed a great meal with Joan and Kevin and Frank that evening. Some of the other people who lived and worked there were also present. They were all friendly and welcoming. Everyone treated everyone else like family.

The next day, Clint went to help Frank finish the work on that tractor he had been working on.

Joan showed Sonya how to raise a healthy garden and how to care for the fruit trees. Hannah and Samuel met a few other children of people living and working there and were having a blast playing with these new friends. Rafe and Zola were enjoying their time there as well. The two dogs they had met the day before were keeping them thoroughly entertained. Later on, Joan took Sonya for a walk on one of the nature preserve's hiking trails. Sonya couldn't get over how beautiful and peaceful it was.

That evening, Sonya and her dad were just relaxing by their cabin and talking. Sonya said, "It's so perfect here. I really like this."

He said, "Yeah, I agree. Maybe we should take them up on their offer to live here for good."

"You really think so?" Sonya asked.

"Let's just take it day by day and see how it goes, okay?" he said.

Sonya said, "Okay. Sounds good. I'm really tired. I'm going to go lay down for the night. All the fresh air, working in the garden, and the hike that Joan took me on wore me out."

Clint said, "Same for me. I'm gonna hit the sack, as well. Goodnight, sweetheart."

They both slept like babies all through the night. The next day they helped out with more things around the farm. In the afternoon, the entire group went on a long hike through the nature preserve. There was so much to explore. They saw all kinds of wildlife and beautiful scenery. They were tired and hungry by the time they returned to the farm. They ate, slept and then got up and did it all again the next day. And the next. And the next.

The days turned into weeks. Then the weeks turned into months. Obviously, they had truly settled into this life and found a place to call home. They hadn't experienced any sign of the trouble from the city making it out to where they now were. No one knew how long it would stay this way, but they had high hopes that it would stay peaceful out here forever. They lived every day as if it would and appreciated each other and every minute of their new life.

END